Stoneflight

GEORGESS McHARGUE
Drawings by Arvis Stewart

THE VIKING PRESS NEW YORK

First Edition

Text copyright © 1975 by Georgess McHargue
Illustrations copyright © 1975 by The Viking Press, Inc.
All rights reserved
First published in 1975 by The Viking Press, Inc.
625 Madison Avenue, New York, N.Y. 10022
Published simultaneously in Canada by
The Macmillan Company of Canada Limited
Printed in U.S.A.

1 2 3 4 5 79 78 77 76 75

Library of Congress Cataloging in Publication Data

McHargue, Georgess. Stoneflight.
Summary: Janie uses her power to put life in the stone animals
that ornament New York buildings to escape her parents'
quarreling, but when the animals start to turn her into stone
she learns that having feelings is the price of remaining human.
[1. Family life—Fiction. 2. Fantasy]
I. Stewart, Arvis L., illus. II. Title.
PZ7.M183St [Fic] 74-11146

ISBN 0-670-67107-X

Stoneflight

For George Nicholson and Olga Litowinsky

I

Janie Harris sat on the kitchen counter in the warm, empty apartment. She was picking at the thick, reddish-yellow scab on her knee and deciding not to go outside, although among the faint sounds of West 116th Street in summer she could hear the rhythmic metal-on-sidewalk whirr of roller skates. The scab was from the last time she'd gone skating, when she and Alan and Evalee had been talking so fast she had caught a wheel on a broken place in the sidewalk. It wasn't falling down she cared about, it was being reminded that Alan and Evalee and everyone else she knew in the whole world had gone away for the summer and left her stuck in the city with a lot of *little kids.* Yuck. At least, that was what she told herself now.

The scab was itchy, which Mom said meant the scrape

was getting well. Janie wiggled it hard to stop the itching, and a little corner came off. Now there was blood running down her leg, warm and wet. She reached for a paper towel to mop it up, wondering hopefully whether she might bleed to death right there in the kitchen. However, the blood stopped flowing pretty quickly, leaving only an oozy place that was making a new scab. It was amazing anything could dry out on a day like this. June was famous, in poems anyway, for roses and breezes and blue sky. Instead of which, everything in New York was thick, warm, and sticky. The whole day is like blood, she thought. Just a nasty, *bloody* day.

The sound of a key in the lock meant Janie's mother was home from her afternoon of showing sketches to a client. First came the click of the ordinary door lock, then the crunch, chunk of the big, heavy no-burglars lock. Next was the sound of the portfolio being put down on a chair in the hall, which should have been followed by footsteps heading for the living room or her parents' bedroom. Instead there was the *whump* of the swinging door, and Janie craned her neck around to see her mother come into the kitchen.

"Hello, darling. What in the world are you doing moping in here? Why aren't you outside on a nice day like this?"

A nice day! Janie took her feet out of the sink so her mother could get a drink of water and said flatly, "It's too hot and everything feels gooey." She half expected to be scolded for having her feet where they didn't belong, but Mom just stood there, looking at her over the rim of the yellow plastic kitchen glass. She wasn't mad, Janie decided, just kind of limp. There was a smudge of New York soot on her forehead, her short, reddish-tawny hair looked as if it were too tired to curl, and some colored samples of material were about to fall out of one of the pockets on the brown leather purse she called her saddlebag. Mrs. Harris stood looking at her daughter for a minute, wearing a puzzled expression. As if, Janie thought, she were trying to decide what to do with a piece of furniture that didn't match the rest of the set.

"Janie," said her mother, putting down the glass, "sometimes I just don't know what to do with you." It was becoming a familiar complaint, and Janie saw from her mother's face that she had had the same thought. Her mother shrugged a little and began pushing the escaping samples back into the saddlebag. "Darling, I know it's a little hot today, but it's going to be a lot hotter than this before the summer's over. What happened to all the things you said you were going to do *if only* we wouldn't send you off to camp? Can't you get yourself together and—and cope? That's what people have to do in this life, cope."

Janie put her feet back in the sink and turned on the water so that it ran over her toes. "I am coping," she said, not looking at her mother. "I'm keeping cool."

"Oh, darling. Honestly. It's only the end of June and if you go on like this much longer you'll get sick. I know. Why don't you go up on the roof, now that they've finally got it fixed? You used to like it up there."

"I can't," said Janie in a bored voice. She was almost enjoying making difficulties now. "Don't you remember? They fixed the roof, but they're still keeping the doors locked so nobody can get in and steal things. There's a sign thing about it in the elevator."

"Is there? Oh yes, I remember. But it says anybody in the building can have a key to the roof from the custodian on request. Go out and ring for the elevator and see if I'm not right."

"Oh, Mom. Do I *have* to?" Janie could just see herself waiting for the elevator and holding the automatic door open while she goggled at the sign. There were sure to be people inside and they would all stare at her as if she were in a glass case at the Museum of Natural History. "Little girl, do you always ring for elevators and then not ride in them?" Unh-unh. No way.

"Yes, you have to. You know you'll like it once you get up there. And if the sign says what I think it does, you can ride right down to Mr. Springstiel's office and ask him *politely* for a key. Say I sent you. If he's not in his office we'll telephone him later."

Janie could tell that Mom had gotten into one of her brisk moods, when she was convinced that everything that was wrong with the world could be fixed if people just got organized. "Come on, now," concluded Mom. "Off you go. I don't want to see you moping around here anymore today."

Janie went, almost fast enough to escape hearing the exasperated call, "And for heaven's sake dry your *feet* and put on some *shoes*! Sometimes I just don't know what to do. . . ." Janie snatched up her sandals, slithered out the door, and headed down the spinach-green hallway for the elevator.

Mom was right about the notice, of course. Mary Morlan Harris was usually right about things like that. Already the paper taped to the elevator wall was dog-eared and covered with little drawings, telephone numbers, peace symbols, slogans, and short words of the kind kids were supposed to pretend they didn't know. Nevertheless, the purple writing could still be read: "Tenants may obtain keys from the custodian," it said in part. Janie pushed the button marked B and went down the cement-floored basement corridor to the little room that was the office of the custodian, Mr. Springstiel. She got the key with no trouble.

From the flat, tarred roof of her building, Janie could see down 116th Street to Columbia University in one direction and across Riverside Drive, the West Side Highway, and Riverside Park to the Hudson River in the other. She had forgotten how good it made you feel to be able to see all that space. The building's tenants had not been allowed to use the roof for more than two years because part of the parapet that ran around the edge had been creaky and unsafe. After a lot of complaints, the parapet had been fixed.

The way onto the roof was through a little hut-shaped structure with a slanting back that stood up from the middle of the roof. Janie scrambled up the slanting back of the stairway access so she could check out the ventilating pipe that stood like a small chimney beside it.

Three years ago a sparrow had made a nest in the pipe, and Janie and her friend Evalee had spent a lot of time watching the scrawny, scrawking babies and trying to feed them. The nest had been much too far down in the pipe for them to reach, so they had dropped all sorts of things into it, from popcorn to hamburger. Although the sparrow babies had paid no attention at all to this rain of food, the two girls had been convinced they were saving the nestlings from starvation. Then they had told Janie's father about the nest because he was a science teacher (and an English teacher too), and maybe he would know what to feed sparrows. Instead, he had taken them up on the roof one morning and showed them how, if they sat very still, they could see the mother bird feed the babies herself. Janie grinned as she remembered how sure the two of them had been that the little sparrows would die if they weren't fed by human beings.

This year, however, the ventilator pipe was empty. She sat down on the edge of the roof and absentmindedly brushed the gritty New York soot from her jeans.

Everything she could see, even the building across the street, was blurred by the summer haze. It seemed to fill up the spaces between the buildings like warm soup. Six stories below her a convertible was waiting for the light, its top down and its radio blaring. "Wind from the southeast at four miles per hour," it said. "Temperature eighty-six degrees, relative humidity ninety-eight per cent. Tomorrow partly sunny and warm; temperatures in the mid-eighties. We repeat the first news item. . . ."

Ninety-eight per cent humidity. It sure felt like it. Janie knew there was some reason why 98 per cent humidity didn't mean the air was 98 per cent water, but she never seemed to remember what it was. Sometimes humidity could even be 100 per cent and still the city wasn't drowned. Wouldn't it be a wild thing, though, if the air *were* water? Nice, cool water. Then she'd be sitting on an island, or better still a reef. The cars on the street would be crabs scuttling on the sea bottom and she, Janie, would be a small, adventurous fish. When she swam, the flare of her bell-bottoms would even make a tail. She'd slide smoothly off her roof and down the canyon of 116th Street, looking in everybody's windows and swimming in among the four twisted columns that held up the overhang of number 643 across the street. She'd scratch her scales on the green leaves of the trees on the Columbia campus and then just swim on out of this summer altogether, back to last winter or into the next one. Last winter would be better—when Mom and Dad still seemed to like each other. She'd be an ice fish, swimming under a crystal roof. She'd—*she'd slip if she didn't watch herself!* Sitting on the flat front part of the stairway access, she had leaned so far out, arms on knees, that she had slid forward several inches. Not only that, she could hear footsteps in the metal stairwell beneath her. She didn't want to get caught sitting over the door. Like most interesting things, it probably wasn't allowed. Should she just jump down onto the main roof? It looked awfully far, and besides, she would make a very loud thump. Whoever was coming would be bound to ask what she'd been doing, especially if it were Mr. Springstiel.

Janie was about to wriggle herself down the slope behind her when she heard something else and relaxed. "La, la, la-*la*, la-la, la-*la*, la-*la*." Only her father half whistled, half hummed that tune like that. It was from a movie called *Doctor Zhivago* that she'd been too young to be interested in. But Dad hummed it all the time and whenever anybody, like Mom, asked him why, he'd just say, "Well, it goes on and on without coming to an end, so I never have to worry about remembering the beginning."

Janie's blue-clad legs were hanging down in front of the open door. Her father didn't seem to notice anything, however, until he'd walked almost all the way through the door and her legs were up against his shoulders. The whistle-humming stopped short. "Good grief!" said Dad, staring straight ahead. "Some mysterious personage has just kicked me in the clavicles. Who can it possibly be?"

"It's me," said Janie. "I mean, it's the Great Flying

Fleagle. I'm walking in the air getting my football practice. What are your clavicles?"

Her father put up his hands and took hold of her ankles. "The clavicles are the collarbones, as any Fleagle should know. Are you coming down, or are you going to go on flying?"

She wriggled farther forward on the roof so that more of her legs hung down her father's chest. "Carry me. Give me a ride the way you used to when I was little."

"Carry you! Good grief, child, have you any idea what you weigh these days? Don't my aging shoulders carry burdens enough? Come on, I'll lift you down instead." He turned around, raised his arms, and swung her to the ground, holding her by the waist. It seemed to Janie that he didn't have any trouble doing it, so why hadn't he wanted to carry her? Sometimes grownups seemed to enjoy talking as if they were falling apart. She thought about that as she followed him over to the parapet.

For a while they stood side by side, looking west across the river, where the sun was going down like an old brass subway token. It was still warm out, but there was definitely a breeze, and it smelled of something besides hot road surface. Up above the Palisades the haze was turning its usual sunset pink. Somehow it didn't remind Janie of blood the way it would have a while ago. She had her arms clasped around one of the roughly triangular stone decorations that formed the top of the parapet. You couldn't see it from this side, of course, but she knew that the pieces were carved with flowers and curly leaves, one with flowers, one with leaves, one with flowers again, all the way across the building and around the courtyard. Her fingers told her this one was a leaf one. Maybe, just maybe, the summer would be bearable after all. If she could learn not to hear the wrong things and think about the wrong things . . .

"Jan-Jan," said her father. He was using his "official" voice, the one for parent-type subjects. Uh-oh, Mom must have told him he had to come and talk to her. "Jan-Jan, I think we ought to have a talk about you and this summer. Now, you know things didn't work out just the way we'd have liked. If we had known beforehand that Gram wasn't going to feel well enough to have us on the Island this year, well, maybe we could have planned ahead a little. But since I had this paper to write, your mother and I took you at your word when you insisted you'd rather stay in the city than go to camp. We thought you were old enough to make up your own mind. Right now I'm beginning to think we were wrong. You really can't mope around all day. It's not good for you, and it's making your mother worry. What happened to all those things you were so anxious to do?"

Something cold clenched itself in Janie's stomach, and she squeezed up hard against the piece of stone she was clasping. She should have figured this was coming. What could she possibly say? Knowing it was a mistake, she came out with the first thing she could think of.

"How can I find anything to do when Alan and Evalee went off to visit their old cousin in Wisconsin when they weren't supposed to? Everything that was going to happen this summer was something we were going to do *together*." Dad was looking straight at her with his mouth pulled in and his jaw stuck forward, the way he did when he was really paying attention. That didn't make it any easier, so Janie hurried on before he could interrupt. "And then the people at the art school wouldn't let me into their silly sculpture class thing when they found out I wasn't fourteen. Why did they call it a children's class, anyway? And I can't make anything big with clay at home because Mom says it's too messy to keep it damp and the bathroom really is too small." She had stopped looking at her father and was pretending to be very interested in a pigeon that was coasting down toward a windowsill across the street. In one minute he was going to say there must be other friends of hers who had stayed in New York for the summer and there were still plenty of things to do in the park. The park! She chewed the inside of her lower lip. Then she felt Dad's arm around her. He gave her a small shake and a squeeze.

"Well, well. Jan-Jan, I know it's not easy. We'll have to think of something. Now skip on downstairs. Mother told me to tell you dinner's almost ready. This summer simply isn't going as planned."

Janie was just ducking into the stairway entrance, feeling slightly relieved, when she heard him add, as if to himself, "It sure isn't."

17

2

It was the middle of the night before Janie remembered Griff. She woke up to find that the room had gotten cooler and she needed to pull up the summer blanket. Then, as she lay watching the lights of passing cars make sliding, slatty patterns on the ceiling, it came to her that when she was on the roof she hadn't even looked at the big stone statue of a griffin that stood at one corner of the parapet. Before, when she and Evalee had played up there, they had named him Griff and dared each other to climb up to him. That had been three years ago, however, when they were practically babies. Janie was sure that now she could find a way to climb all that way. It would be exciting to sit up there and it wouldn't even be *very* dangerous, because ever since they had built the high-rise apartment next door, there was a solid brick wall going straight up beside Griff's left wing.

The best thing about sitting on Griff would be that it was absolutely private. Even if somebody should come up on the roof, chances were she'd never be noticed. It might not be as cool as sitting with your feet in the sink, but there wouldn't be any interruptions. Janie knew she *had* to make some sort of plan for the rest of the summer, had to think about what would happen if her parents really decided not to live together anymore. Only, what good would it do to *think* about that, when there was nothing she could *do* about it? Probably it was better to pretend she was as dumb as they seemed to think. At least she'd have to figure out a way to look busy because the more she was noticed, these days, the worse things got.

By now she was all the way awake. She writhed down to the window at the foot of the bed and put her head out. There on the third floor the street lights shone bright as moonlight. The haze was too thick for more than a couple of stars to show through, and she thought how there might be real moonlight at Gram's house on Dixon's Island. Nevertheless, it was bright enough for her to see across some of the crazy, carved front of her own building. Everything was curly—the upside-down-V-shaped things over the windows, the line of stone panels that went up the front of the building at each corner, and especially the top and sides of the doorway inside the courtyard. If you looked carefully, you could see that the best part of all that carving was that it was crazy. It was all meant to be plants, but they certainly weren't like anything anybody ever saw in a fruit market or a florist's. There were big things like tulips that seemed to have roses inside them, lilies that grew out of clusters of oak leaves, apples the size of grapefruits, clumps of things like strawberries, branches that were half pine and half maple, giant violets, and things that looked like crosses between pears and bananas. It was weird, all right, but Janie liked it. It was even better from across the street. Then you could see the whole front, including the toothy carvings on the edge of the roof and Griff, standing proudly on his pedestal at the west corner. The strange thing was that there wasn't another griffin at the east corner, although there was another pedestal. Mom had told her once that old Mrs. Gottschalk said the builder ran out of money before the building was finished.

Janie craned farther out her window, not caring about the black soot that would get on her pajamas from the sill. But although she practically twisted her neck off peering upward, she couldn't lean out far enough to see Griff without having her head and stomach feel funny. She wriggled onto the bed, dusted herself off rather messily, and got back under the covers. She slept soundly and dreamed about being a goldfish in a warm round bowl.

The next morning, Janie managed to avoid any further talk about the summer by waiting to get up until she heard her parents finish breakfast. Then she knew her father would go off to the Columbia University Library to work on his paper, "Administrative Aspects of Interim Funding of the New York City Public Schools," and Mom would be busy making lists of things that had to be done later. Janie got herself a large bowl of Froot Loops with milk and canned peaches, even though she knew her parents would rather have her eat organic cereal. (Janie thought Granola tasted like the stuff Gram fed her golden bantam hens.) She finished breakfast and made it out the front door just before Mom came into the kitchen to make a list of what they needed for dinner.

Up on the roof, Janie headed straight for Griff's corner. The stone griffin stood on a gray stone pedestal that rose about three feet above the top of the decorated stone parapet. Janie stood several feet away and looked at him carefully. Griffins, of course, were half lion and half falcon. She had read about them in a book from the library that told all about the imaginary animals in old myths and legends. This griffin somehow looked especially real. The lion parts of him (his body, legs, and tail) fitted so well with the falcon parts (the head, neck, and wings) that it became hard to remember that actual falcons had only two legs with talons and actual lions had manes and cat faces with whiskers. Like all proper griffins, Griff also had tall, pointed ears, although nothing of the sort had ever been seen on either a lion or a falcon.

Very straight the stone griffin stood, looking out over the street as if he were guarding the building. His wings were held up over his back, his hooked beak looked sharp and determined, and his lion's tail with the tassel on the end was curled gracefully around his right hind leg.

"Hello, old griffin," said Janie in her mind. "How have you been for two years? Thank goodness you haven't grown as much as I have." But getting up on Griff's back wasn't going to be easy, even now, she saw. The pedestal he stood on was completely smooth, unlike almost anything else on the building.

Even if she got up to the edge there would still be a yard of smooth stone to climb before she stood on a level with Griff.

Janie sat down on the roof and chewed an end of her hair while she thought. The whole thing would be perfectly simple if she had a ladder or a lot of crates to make steps. No way. She remembered her mother saying that everything that was fun was illegal, immoral, or fattening. That was a grown-up joke. Well, there weren't very many things she, Janie, wanted to do that were either illegal or immoral (except lying about her age to get into the movies—or a sculpture class). And she didn't seem to get fat, no matter what she ate. But Janie knew, from more than ten years of experience, that almost anything a kid thought of to do was either dangerous, impolite, or just plain not allowed. Evalee had a saying that covered the situation: "Ask first and miss out." (Evalee had a whole notebook of sayings like that; she called them Survival Sayings.) Okay. No big ladders to attract attention. And no grown-up help.

Janie went back down to the apartment very slowly, not walking on the stairs but putting her sneakered feet inside the slanting spaces between the metal banister bars. To do this she had to lean quite far over the handrail and look down the stairwell. She stared at the oblong of specked stone lobby floor five flights below her, watching it get bigger as she went down to her own floor, the third. She was imagining that the stairwell was the street and that she was standing on the edge of the parapet beside Griff's pedestal. Winding herself down the zigzag spiral of the stairwell, she thought she could feel the stairs and the building itself growing down from her feet, not only to ground level but below it—down to the basement, and the rock and dirt beneath it, down through miles and miles of earth to the red-hot part in the middle where the rocks were liquid. It was strange that, instead of making her feel dizzier, the thought made her feel safer. She was connected to the planet, as much a part of it as its whole crust, the island of Manhattan, and one rather rickety apartment house that stuck up from West 116th Street.

But how would she feel if the banister weren't there to lean over? *That* wouldn't be nearly so much fun.

Janie wore her own set of keys to the apartment (and now the roof) around her neck on a string. She slipped in her front door quietly. Just at this point, she decided,

23

she really didn't want to meet her mother. If she were going to climb up to Griff without help then it had better be a real secret. It would at least make something to write Evalee and Alan about. She had already gotten one letter from them, six pages long because Alan had written it in his enormous eight-year-old writing. The letter had been mostly a long list of super-fantastic things Alan and Evalee had done on their cousin's farm, which was also super-fantastic (to use Alan's favorite word). Evalee had just added a short postscript at the end. Everything was okay, she said, but riding the farm horses hadn't really been all that much fun and Monster Face (that was Alan) had actually fallen off once. Janie understood that Evalee was feeling sorry about having deserted her, Janie, in hot old New York, but she hadn't been able to get herself together and write back.

By now, Janie had finished making the beds, which was her chore that week. She was really supposed to have done it earlier, but she knew Mom would not have been around to check on her yet. That was the advantage of having that sort of parent—you always knew what a really organized person was likely to be doing when. Not that Mary Harris had been *born* organized, Janie knew. "When I was young I had about the most scattered brains in Massachusetts," her mother was fond of saying, "but with the life I lead, I simply had to learn to be organized. I wear so many hats I need a hatrack to keep them all straight."

When Janie was little, she had wondered what Mom meant by that, because actually she hardly ever wore any hat at all. The most she ever put on her head was a scarf with the designer's name on it. By now, though, Janie knew her mother meant she ought to have several kinds of hats because she had several jobs. She needed a businesswoman hat for Mary Harris, president of Mary Morlan Harris, Inc., Interior Decoration and Design, and then she needed an artist's beret for being the entire design staff of the corporation and a chef's cap and a general mother hat for cleaning house, finding lost sweaters, and putting Band-Aids on scraped knees. Of course sometimes, just sometimes, the decorator's hat would forget to buy any meat sauce to go on top of the spaghetti, or the mother hat (a sort of pioneer woman's sunbonnet, Janie thought) would tidy away an important sketch and not be able to find it again. "What about the wife hat?" Dad would tease. "Oh, that one. Well, darling, that one's on all the time, underneath the others." Right at this minute, however, Janie's mother would be in the kitchen, wearing either her mother hat for putting things in the dishwasher or her business-woman hat for telephoning clients about appointments and fabric samples. This left Janie free to make an inconspicuous tour of the building.

She knew from years of delightful discoveries that the trash cans outside apartment back doors were as good as a Treasure Isle and second-hand store combined. In less than fifteen minutes she had found what she was looking for. Outside the door of 1K sat a perfectly sturdy wooden crate containing two bags of garbage and a lot of scrunched-up raffia. Beside it lay its top and a long piece of light rope.

She carried her loot back to the apartment and stowed the crate temporarily behind her bed. She wanted to find her pocketknife, the one Uncle Arthur had sent her from Switzerland. Unfortunately, however, the knife seemed to have disappeared. Well, then, she'd have to have a knife from the kitchen, since she was likely to want to cut her cord and scissors would never do it. But Mom was hardly going to say, "Yes, darling, of course you may have one of my big kitchen knives to play with so you can cut off all your fingers and ruin the blade." Not likely. "Ask first and miss out," as Evalee would say. But another one of the Survival Sayings might be even more use now. It was, "Nobody stops a kid who's trying to be helpful." Janie went into the kitchen, waved when her mother craned her neck around the telephone cord to see who it was, and began unloading the breakfast dishes from the dishwasher. Clash, clash, clash. Plates in a stack for Mom to put up on the top shelf. Clink, clink, clink. Juice glasses on the left, milk glasses on the right. Thud for last night's pottery casserole under the counter. Ting, ting for the good stainless in the chest. And finally thung, thung, thung, for the kitchen knives and forks in the drawer by the stove. It was almost too simple to slide one of the sharp paring knives under her shirt, tuck in the dangling tail, mime a silent good-by to her mother from the doorway, and beat it safely down the hall. "Nobody stops a kid who's trying to be helpful." Right on.

Back in her own room, she gathered her gear together. She remembered a TV program she had seen in which a bunch of climbers went up an incredibly tall and difficult mountain near Mount Everest. Carefully, she wrapped her rope around her waist. Then she was reminded of the knife, which felt cold and dangerous against the skin of her stomach. She got it out and stuck it in her belt, or rather into the rope around her middle. Now she felt like a pirate as well as a mountaineer. For a final touch, she got the yardstick out of the hall closet. Using it for a walking stick, she climbed up to the roof again.

Janie's first attempt to act like a mountaineer wasn't very successful. Standing on the crate didn't get her nearly high enough to climb the pedestal. With a dissatisfied grunt, she got down and went to sit in the shade of the stairway access. It was getting hot again and from where she was sitting the statue looked higher and harder to climb than the Himalayas. At least they had a lot of good cold snow on top. If only she were an ant, she could go right up the side of the pedestal. If only she were a cat burglar, she could go right up the cracks between the bricks in the wall of the building next door. Hey, the wall! She had forgotten about the wall that ran up by Griff's left side. It was perfectly sheer, without any windows or ledges, and between it and the parapet of her own building was a scary gap of about two feet. Falling down that would be like falling down the slot in a toaster. But—but, but, but, sputtered Janie in her head like a backfiring engine—the wall wasn't all brick. The corner on the street was made of big blocks of gray stone because the building front was stone. And those stone blocks had big, deep cracks between them. One of those cracks was nearly on a level with the top of the parapet, and it would be the easiest thing in the world to bridge the gap by putting one end of a board into the slot between the blocks. And she had a board.

The top of the crate fitted easily into the slot and there was a good foot of it that jutted inside the parapet. The whole thing felt pretty firm and would give her plenty of room to stand with both feet. Once she had put the crate itself in the angle between the back of the pedestal and the parapet, it was amazing how quickly she found herself up where she wanted to be. One big step to the top of the crate and another one onto the makeshift platform. Next came the real mountaineering part. She doubled her cord (it was really almost as thick as clothesline) and reached up until she could loop it around one of Griff's big stone legs. Now that she had something to grab onto, it was easy to boost herself chest-high onto the top of the pedestal. She lay on her stomach congratulating herself, but only for an instant. The top of the pedestal was far from clean, as she ought to have guessed. It was covered with soot and bird droppings and even some feathers, while old leaves and other bits of trash had blown and been caught around the stone paws. She scrambled to her feet and walked cautiously around to the front of the statue (not too near the edge).

Ooh. Ooh, wow. Janie drew in her breath deep, deep, all the way to her heels. She felt suddenly as if she were made of air, part of the little wind that puffed at her gently from the river. She almost had to slam one arm around the neck of the stone griffin in order to keep from sliding off over the street on that little wind. This was High. This was Up. This was the place where everything was different. Down below she could see the whole street from sidewalk to sidewalk. The people and dogs and cars and buses looked nearer instead of farther away because there was nothing at all between her and them. Even the traffic light on the corner looked brighter and clearer, as if it were a traffic light in some foreign city. And the river, that great, huge river. It wasn't just a nice piece of water at the end of the street, brown or blue or gray according to the weather. Now she could see big stretches of it that she had never noticed before. Now the reddish cliffs of the Palisades on the other shore looked enormous, and below them the Hudson was truly a river, flowing, running, going to the sea, pushing yellowish foam against the paint-blotched freighter and two strings of barges that were churning their way slowly upstream.

Yesterday Janie had imagined herself a fish swimming

in the sea that filled the canyons of New York. Today she felt she was in a sailboat skimming the top of that sea and peering down through its clear water.

She might have stood for days looking out over West 116th Street, stood there until winter came and froze her into stone beside the griffin, if her left arm hadn't begun to get a cramp in it. With a sigh, she stepped back and rubbed the inside of her arm. It was all printed with red and white feather marks from the stone neck. The arm was pretty grubby, too. Janie realized that before she could really enjoy her new observation post she would have to get busy with soap and water. A little soot was all right, but she drew the line at bird droppings.

For the third time that day she went down the echoing stairway, absentmindedly picking a feather off her front as she went. A quick survey of the kitchen revealed the usual selection of things for lunch. She settled on a leftover deviled egg, a thick, oozy peanut butter and Spam sandwich, and an orange popsicle from the freezer. While she was getting this together, she decided to have a picnic on the roof, so she ate the already melting popsicle first while she collected the whisk broom, an old torn sheet from the rag bag, and a big bottle of Lestoil. At the last minute she added a can of cherry soda to her load. Then she headed back to the roof.

She giggled to herself as she wondered what her picnic would have looked like to somebody else. She could see herself all bright and flickery on a TV screen.

"I always drink refreshing Lestoil with my lunch, for shinier teeth and a cleaner stomach." Or maybe: "After scrubbing my kitchen with Lestoil I always polish up with a Skippy's Peanut Butter sandwich. For cleaning, nothing's as zippy as Skippy." Maybe, too, you could mix cherry soda and Lestoil—it wasn't any stranger than some kinds of cocktails.

In the end, Janie wasn't so sure Lestoil was quite the thing to use for cleaning stone griffins, however. The whisk broom was pretty good for removing loose dirt, but it didn't do a thing for the black city soot that had been collecting on the stone for years. Rubbing at it with a piece of old sheet soaked in the Lestoil did get some of the dirt off, but it also seemed to spread it around so that the dark streaks made by the rain began to turn into a general gray color. It was hard, hot work, but she stuck with it.

As she scrubbed at the rough stone she noticed things about the way the griffin had been carved. He was really an extra nice griffin with all the parts of him exactly right. You could see the fur curling on the backs of his legs and between his toes, and the insides of his front feet even had those two extra claws that didn't touch the ground, just like her Uncle Arthur's cat Maxim. The griffin's face was unusual, too. Janie didn't know very much about the shape of real falcons' faces, so she couldn't be sure how much the person who had made the statue was inventing. He (or she, Janie reminded herself—think of Louise Nevelson) had given this falcon very expressive eyebrows—ridges of feathers over his eyes that curved up and out at the ends. When you looked at his face the right way, you saw that though he could be fierce if he wanted to and though he was very proud of being so big and strange and powerful, he also knew perfectly well that he was just a decoration on a run-down old building in a city where most people had never heard of a griffin. Probably, she thought, he also knew a lot about the people who lived in that city; he'd had a long time to watch them. She wasn't sure how old the building was, but she knew Mrs. Gottschalk from 4H had told Mom that she and Mr. Gottschalk had lived in that same apartment ever since they came to America in 1927. Griff had stood there for more than forty-five years, at least.

Janie hauled herself up from her crouched position and stretched her back and shoulders. She seemed to have been brushing and scrubbing for weeks but she felt wonderful. She leaned back contentedly against Griff's shoulder, just at the place where the feathers gave way to fur. Up between the wings, she had noticed, was the perfect place to sit, almost like a throne with the incurved wings for back and arms. She didn't think she would climb up there right now, however. She was on the shaded side of the griffin and the stone was cool behind her. The sound of traffic from the street had fallen into an afternoon lull. She almost thought she could feel its vibration coming up through her feet and through the stone behind her. Like a cat purring. Did griffins purr? Janie decided this one did.

3

All at once, Janie felt very energetic. She gathered up her cleaning equipment, slithered quickly but carefully down to the surface of the roof, and galloped back down to the apartment. She had had an idea. Mom wasn't going to be back till late because she was presenting plans for remodeling a "terribly interesting town house" in Brooklyn. She hated subways and would probably be tired and hot when she got home. This time, however, she was going to have a wonderful surprise waiting for her. Janie was going to set the table and get the dinner all ready herself.

She knew that getting dinner that night wouldn't be all that difficult. There was cold chicken left from Wednesday, so all that really had to be done was to make some salad and set the table. Still, it would look very impressive to have things all done by the time Mom got home. She decided she would make this a real occasion and set the oak dining table instead of the kitchen one where they usually ate.

It was while she was making the salad, which only meant tearing up some lettuce, that Janie had her other idea. She would make a chocolate roll for dessert. That would make her father happy because Mom hardly ever made desserts on account of not getting too fat. ("Just be glad that at my age I still have a figure to worry about," she would say whenever Dad told her not to fret.) Nevertheless, Janie knew she loved sweet things and always ate as much as anyone whenever Uncle Arthur came to dinner and brought one of his homemade tarts. Uncle Arthur worked for a big importing company and always told such amazing stories about his trips to places like Finland and Zambia. This would be like those times, when everyone laughed and talked and spent a long time at the dinner table.

Janie put the salad in the icebox and went to get a chair so she could reach the chocolate wafers. They were at the very back of the top shelf because they had been bought last spring when Barbara-from-Barnard had shown her how to make a chocolate roll.

That was one of the nice things about Barbara-from-Barnard, who was her last year's babysitter. (Once there had been another Barbara, called Barbara-from-Hunter-College, but she had gotten married and moved to Ohio.) *This* Barbara not only made chocolate roll but let Janie stay up as late as she wanted to because she, Barbara, refused to become a "tool of oppression" and "perpetuate the hierarchical values of society." The only thing Janie understood about that was that it meant not making people do what they didn't want to do. If the result was that she could stay up for the late movie, that was fine by Janie, but it was closely connected to the bad thing about Barbara. You couldn't talk about anything to Barbara without having her bring up something called the Class Struggle. The Class Struggle was what all Barbara's courses seemed to be about, even required chemistry. (Barbara said it was repressive of the college to make her take chemistry, but it was useful in the end because it showed you how scientists thought they were above the Class Struggle even though they weren't really.) In the end Janie got pretty tired of the Class Struggle and was even a little glad when vacation came and she knew she wouldn't be able to see the late movie again until September.

The way Barbara made chocolate roll looked incredibly easy. All you had to do was take a box of thin, round chocolate cookies and make an enormous sandwich out of them with Reddi-Wip or some other kind of whipped-creamy stuff that fizzed out of a can. You made the sandwich in a bread tin with the cookies standing up on edge and then you frosted the whole thing over with more cream on the outside. When you were done you left the roll in the icebox for at least an hour and it mysteriously turned into thin layers of cake with frosting between.

In practice, the recipe turned out to be a little more difficult and messier than Janie remembered. Each stack of frosted cookies was as hard to handle as a pile of phonograph records with shaving cream between them. The cookies were very brittle, too, and she had a hard time not breaking all their edges. The outside of the roll went better, however. There was plenty of cream in the can, so she could experiment. The can had come with several little nozzles of different shapes and Janie used them to make designs all over the top of the roll, just like a wedding cake in a bakery window. It was really fun, once she learned how to keep her hand steady and not make the cream come out in whooshes. There were helpful instructions on the can, which told her to try out each nozzle on a piece of waxed paper first. That was obviously a good idea. In some ways the paper was even more interesting to draw on than the cake. She made a cat with whiskers and a party hat and was about to put a pompon on the hat when she remembered what she was really doing. There was just enough stuff to finish off the end of the chocolate roll. Then the nozzle gave an apologetic wheeze, spat out some thin white goo, and gave up altogether.

Nevertheless, Janie was satisfied. The roll was amazing, rosetted, frilled, and swirled like the carved front of her own building after a heavy snow. She put it proudly in the refrigerator and was astonished to see that it was five forty. Wow, Mom would be home any minute and the dinner table wasn't quite finished. It wasn't just going to be set, it was going to have dinner already on it, so when her mother walked in she would know right away what a remarkable daughter she had. Out came the cold chicken, the dish with the leftover stuffing, and the salad.

She had just time to get out the salad oil and the vinegar when she heard her mother come in.

"Darling, is that you?" called Mom from the hall. "Come out and give me a kiss."

"I can't," she called back. "I'm just setting the table."

"You're what? Why, Janie, how nice. Let me get these vile shoes off and I'll be right out." Her voice trailed off toward the bedroom.

Janie put down the oil and vinegar carefully and stood beside the dining table. She thought of following Mom into the bedroom to hear about the new townhouse. Usually she was very interested in the places her mother was decorating. She had visited several of them "before and after," and it was more fun than playing dollhouses to see how the right color on the walls or a widened doorway or a new kind of lighting could change a room as completely as if the place had been torn down and rebuilt. It was something like what had happened when she first stood beside Griff today: it made everything look new and free and filled with a different kind of life. This townhouse, Mom said, was a real delight because it was filled with things from the time it was built, in the last century. It had heavy varnished woodwork, tall mirrors, little arched fireplaces for gas fires, and molded plaster walls. Unfortunately, it was also dark, full of small, useless rooms, and falling apart inside. The trick, the thing a good decorator should try to do, was to save the nice parts like the old woodwork and the plaster and still make it into a comfortable house for a modern family. "It isn't any fun to live in a museum," Mom always said, and Janie agreed, remembering places like the Metropolitan Museum where there were velvet ropes across all the furniture.

The edge of the dining table was pressing into the small of Janie's back. What in the world was Mom doing in the bedroom all this time? Didn't she care that the table was set, the dinner was ready, and there was *homemade* dessert waiting in the icebox? Janie stared sternly at the table, wondering whether she'd forgotten anything, but salt, pepper, napkins, plates, glasses, all stared back at her like good children who'd finished their homework. She heard somebody come into the room behind her. "La, la, la-*la, la*-la, la-*la,* la-*la.*" It was Dad, not Mom. He was humming cheerfully as he put down the old college bookbag he still used to carry his notes back and forth.

Janie thought, just for a second, that she might play it cool—act as if there were nothing unusual about the evening and wait for Dad to notice the dinner table. Then she knew she wouldn't do that, because her legs were already pounding across the living room and in two seconds she had banged herself against him as if he were a tree or a lamp post and thrown her arms around his ribs. "Dad, look, guess what! Isn't it gorgeous? I set the table *and* got the dinner ready for Mom all by my-self. *And,*" she added, stepping back and speaking im-pressively, "we're going to have *three courses.*"

"Ooof," said her father, pretending to stagger. "Jan-Jan, you've got to learn not to assault people like that, even with such spectacular news. Now what's this about dinner? Come and show me." He allowed himself to be led to the table. "Beautiful," he declared. "I don't know what more anyone could want on a warm June evening. Except—" He grinned as he saw her face fall. "Except a freezing cold bottle of beer, my little Escoffier. Let's go into the kitchen and get me a beer. My throat is full of library dust."

Janie was not to be sidetracked. "What's an Ess-coff-yay?" They were in the kitchen, and she paused for the *punkle-rrripp-pfff* of the pop-top beer can. She got out a glass and held it slantwise the way he had taught her, so the beer would pour down the side of the glass without having the foam overflow. "Escoffier," answered her father, "was a famous French chef, a master cook. He cooked such wonderful food that any cook would be proud to be called an Escoffier. Any-body knows that." He spoke over his shoulder as he reached down a bag of pretzels from the high cabinet over the refrigerator.

"But Dad, you know I'm taking Spanish, not French. I don't know anything French except little bits of that song you sing about the blond lady, and you won't even tell me what the chorus means. Can I have a pretzel? I didn't know those were up there."

Deftly, her father hoisted the pretzels out of her reach. He picked her up with one arm around her middle, so that he was carrying her into the living room like a folded raincoat. "Jan-Jan, you'll never make the school debating team (that is, if they had a debating team) unless you learn to stick to the point. You raise three topics and I will go after them in order. First: every civilized person should know French and furthermore, as I am about to show you, anyone who knows Spanish and English already knows a little French. You may have a pretzel as soon as you riddle me this riddle—what's Spanish and French too? Second: you are at least three years too young to have me explain that particular, very French song. And third: of course you didn't know those pretzels were up there. With you around all day, a man could starve on what he finds to eat when he gets home. You make a plague of grasshoppers look like picky eaters. In fact," he added, heaving her onto the sofa so that she landed with her ankles beside her ears, "you're getting to be quite an armload. Now, about that riddle."

Five minutes later, they had established that there really were a lot of Spanish words Janie knew that were almost the same in French: *bebé* in Spanish and *bébé* in French, for instance, or *bandido* and *bandit*, *poema* and *poème*, *mamá* and *maman*. "Now," said Dad, "tell me one very important thing that's true of all those pairs of words." He dangled a pretzel temptingly from one finger but Janie wasn't going to be teased. Let's see—all the words were short (no); some had accents and some didn't (no); none of them was very hard. . . . "Hey!" she yelped, pounding her heels on the back of the sofa, "they're not only like each other, they're like English too. *Baby, bandit, poem, mamma.*"

"And so?"

"What do you mean, *and so?* Come on, that's not fair."

"I mean why do you think those three languages have similar words? Is it just an accident?"

"Oh. Well, I suppose they must come from the same beginning, hunh? Like Spanish comes from Latin or something. *Now* can I have that pretzel?" In fact, she already had the pretzel, having hooked it neatly off his finger like the brass ring at the merry-go-round. Ump-tee-tee, ump-tee-tee, ump-tee-tee went the merry-go-round music in her head, the way it had that first summer at Gram's when the carnival came to Harmonport. She'd been too little to reach the ring then. . . .

"Well! What are you two doing?" asked Mom as she came into the living room. She had changed into a pair of seersucker pants and a flowered shirt. She looked pretty and cool but she was looking hard at Dad and something in her voice made Janie start talking too fast.

"I'm learning French," she explained, sliding down to the floor within reach of the pretzels. "That is, Dad is showing me all about how French is like Spanish and English too because they both came from Latin and—"

"Showing you *how*, darling, not *about how*," corrected Mom. "Aren't you home a little early, Ken?"

Janie felt the air go tight, as if there were wires strung through the room, but Dad's voice sounded perfectly ordinary when he answered. "Early? I guess maybe. I finished up with the '65 tax reports and didn't want to start on something else. How about you? Have a good day?"

Janie had become a piece of furniture, an end table slightly out of place on the scratchy gold carpet. She usually found it was better that way. Nobody sent a table out of the room or expected it to react to what went on. It would be *much* better, of course, if she were really made of wood or stone and all her relatives were trees or rocks in some forgotten forest.

"*Good?*" asked Mary Harris, looking away. "I don't know. I lost the townhouse, that's all. They've decided they don't want to preserve it, they want to gut it and do it over in Early Swedish Men's Room. They didn't even have the decency to tell me before I'd finished the sketches."

"Now look. Now look here, Molly." The second time Dad said it he sounded angry. "I'm sorry about the job. I had no idea. There'll be another one. But it's no reason why you can't lay off *me* for just five seconds. I thought we'd been all through that. Come on, now. Fix yourself a Scotch, sit down and have a pretzel, join the human race."

Mom drew in her breath slowly and let it out as if she were throwing away something spoiled.

From the floor the piece of furniture that was their

daughter Janie saw her chance and dived in. Once she reminded them of her presence, she knew her parents would probably drop their argument and pretend that nothing had happened, even seem grateful that she had interrupted them. "Hey, maybe nobody should eat any more pretzels. Just wait till you see what I made for dessert. Come on, Mom, you haven't even looked at the table yet."

"Jan-Jan," said Dad, "how about letting your mother sit down for a minute? She's tired."

"Oh, no. No woman is ever too tired to look at a table set by someone else. And while I'm out there I think I'll fix that Scotch."

The dining table was found to be perfect. "That was very sweet of you, dear, and there isn't a spoon out of place." Her mother gave her a one-armed hug. "Now, what else did you do today? You were very busy this morning, I was glad to see."

"Oh, nothing much. Wait right there by the bar; I'll get the ice for you." Janie had suddenly remembered that she didn't want Mom to spoil the surprise by looking in the icebox. She gave a good hard jerk to the ice tray to get it out and then a really hard wham on the counter to loosen the cubes. All the cutlery rattled in the drawer and cold splinters jumped out of the tray. It was as satisfying as breaking glass.

The drink was made, Dad settled down with a new copy of *Science* and Janie was sent off to wash before dinner. She went without the usual protest, having remembered the amount of soot she had been wallowing in all day. She had changed out of her griffin-washing clothes and given herself a swipe with a washcloth earlier, but even so, a surprising amount of grime came off her face, arms, and neck. Oh, well, the rest could wait till she took her bath.

Somehow, doing so much washing reminded Janie that this was a special occasion. Everything was going to be fine, just the way she had planned. Who could fight at such a beautifully set table?

During dinner the conversation was mostly about a letter Mom had gotten that day from some friends Janie didn't know. She let her mind wander ahead to the moment when her parents would be through with the salad, and she could bring out her wonderful home-made dessert.

Dessert! Hey, she had missed something. Mom was talking to her. "I said, I think we're all through now, darling. Did you say you'd made something special for dessert?"

"You'll see, you'll see," she promised mysteriously, already on her way to the kitchen with the first load of plates. (Remember not to take too many at once. Evalee's Saying Number Eight was, "Being polite is not very efficient.")

The chocolate roll was almost as remarkable looking as she had remembered it was. A few of the swirls and curlicues of frosting had slumped a little, but it was still—

"Great Scott, Jan-Jan," exclaimed Dad. "It's a wedding cake."

"Do you really like it?" she asked, knowing she was fishing for compliments and not caring one bit.

"Like it? Certainly not." She saw he was teasing now. "Does one *like* Mount Everest? Does one *like* the Taj Mahal? No. One admires."

"Heavens, Ken, how you do go on." Mom was moving things to make room on the table. "Not that it isn't a marvelous creation. I'm wildly impressed. From now on we can both retire and keep her chained in the kitchen where she'll do the most good. Janie, I think in this case the cook should do the serving. I'll get the dessert plates."

Janie was holding the cake server over the roll, trying to decide how big a piece she could cut without being a complete pig.

"Hey, Mom, you only got two plates!"

"Oh, but baby, you know I never eat things like that. If I did I'd get so fat Daddy wouldn't want to be seen with me. I thought you made it for him. I'll just sit here and admire it."

"Aaaaw." Janie heard herself making the childish noise and knew instantly what would happen. She was fussing, which was one of the "things we don't do."

"Now, now," said Dad in his *reasonable* voice, "we don't fuss around here. Your mother knows what's best for her diet." His face was bent down over the plate she'd just handed him, but she saw him look up at her and give her half a wink. "Besides, more for us this way. If you'll just pass me that confection of yours, I know I'm going to have to have another piece."

"Sure, Dad." She ate some of her own slice and stared at the streak of late sun that was inching its way across the oak table and the yellow place mats she had thought looked so pretty. She had gone far away into a flat golden world beyond feeling hurt or angry. But she was not so far that she didn't hear her father speaking in a low, neutral voice. "You didn't have to do that, Molly." Again, it was the voice grownups used when they were pretending to be alone. They were so wrapped up in their own made-up world they didn't care what happened in her real one.

In the same tone, but with anger, her mother replied. "Do what? How do you know? You don't know *a goddamned thing* about what I have to do."

Janie dropped her napkin on the table and headed for the kitchen, carrying the remains of the wonderful chocolate roll.

4

Sometime earlier that afternoon (it seemed a year ago now) Janie had thought she might finish off the day by doing the dishes all by herself instead of just helping. Right now, however, the kitchen was the last place she wanted to be.

"Dumb," said a shrill little voice in her head. "You're acting dumb. Like a kid. Ouch." (That last was because she'd hurt her heel kicking shut the door of her room.) Even with the window open it smelled stuffy, a shut-in New York summer smell of humidity acting on wool rug, soot, disused radiator pipes, and sun-warmed plasticine. She flung herself on the bed just for the pleasure of doing something definite.

It would sure be a long time before she did anything like that for Mom again! Janie tried hard to keep feeling angry because it made her feel better, but she couldn't push down the hurtful thoughts. *She could have tasted it. Just a little piece. I wanted her to like it. And*—here came the anger back again—*she isn't fat anyway; she's beautiful. I'll never be that beautiful. She could have tasted it.*

After a long, draggy time she stopped feeling as if her stomach were a load of laundry in an automatic washer. Except for the noise of traffic and the distant, rubbery *sproing* of dishes going into the dishwasher rack, the room was quiet. She had more than half expected to be summoned to help with the dishes as usual but it was too late for that now. She could hear the water sloshing into the machine and there would be nothing left to do except wipe off the counter.

It was still light outside because it was June. Nevertheless, Janie decided, she would put on her pajamas and get into bed. Soon she was deep in one of her favorite books. It was called *A Wrinkle in Time* and was about two kids whose beautiful, red-haired mother was a chemist and whose father was a physicist who got carried off and trapped by something evil that lived in outer space. There were three wise witches in it, who went off with the children to find their father and bring him back so the family could be together again. But they had to go far away to do it, not just miles but light years. A long . . . long way. Somewhere in the middle of the journey Janie fell asleep, sliding sideways in the bed so that her chin rested on the open pages of the book and a hunk of light brown hair flopped over her eyes.

At first it wasn't a real, roaring nightmare, just a rather bewildering dream. She was traveling in space with the three witches from the book, Mrs. Who, Mrs. Which, and Mrs. Whatsit. She knew it was outer space because the sky was thin, cold, utterly black, and filled with stars and comets that went whizzing by like baseballs. At first the witches were friendly. They had shown her how to fly and it was glorious not to be attached to one particular spot on one particular planet. But the four of them were searching for something—something very important—and it seemed to be getting farther and farther away. "Riddle me this riddle," cried the three witches. "Who, which, and what?" But no matter how often Janie guessed, she couldn't get the right answers. "Well, that really takes the cake," declared the witches. "She'll never find out now. Not in English, French, or Spanish. Never, never, never, never." Their voices got smaller and smaller and then she was all alone in the empty universe, staring at one big bright star. It was huge, that star, and square, and yellow. It was a window, not a star. It was a window across the street, and she was awake.

Plain, old familiar sheets under her, solid walls between her and outer space, Big Bear and Baby Bear on the bureau, and the shadow of the old rocking chair on the ceiling, looking, as always, like a cow's head with little knobby horns. Mom must have been in to kiss her and found her asleep because the book was on the bureau now, neatly closed. Janie thought she would get out of bed and look at her shell collection a while. Maybe she'd get a glass of milk from the kitchen, too. Just going to the door felt good. Moving her arms and legs, feeling the floor under her feet, went to prove the dream was over.

She stopped with the door half open. The sound of voices from her parents' bedroom was only a little louder than it had been to her as she lay in bed, since the two rooms were next to each other. Like the traffic, like planes overhead or even the wail of ambulances, fire engines, and police cars, the sound of voices was one of the things you didn't pay much attention to. Except now.

"—typical of the way you always handle any problem. Disregard it, avoid it. Wait for it to go away. That most of all. Well, this time maybe I'll do just that." Mom.

Dad's voice was much lower; she couldn't hear everything he said. "—think you know how unfair— know we agreed to try it your way till the fall term— done my part, certainly." Behind the closed door they sounded strangely stretched and hollow, as if the whole conversation were being printed on the outside of a balloon that was being blown bigger and bigger. Janie slid down to sit on the floor by her own door.

She was a piece of furniture again, absolutely still and unnoticeable. She watched the line of light under the other door and tried to think of nothing at all while the argument swelled up around her. If they didn't want her to hear, why did they talk so loudly? If they did want her to hear, why did they always pretend nothing was wrong when she asked questions? She had stopped asking now, not really wanting to hear something bad and final—like "divorce." But she would still listen, feeling it was better to know what was coming. Now it was mostly her mother talking.

"—stuck in the same place all your life?—can't go on doing the whole thing myself. I can't, I can't." She was crying. Dad said something that was lost in the sound of Kleenex being ripped through the slit in the top of the box. But the answer was sudden and sharp. Mom must have come nearer to the door to get the Kleenex. "Don't you *dare* try to bring Janie into this. That's just an excuse and you know it."

Suddenly the piece of furniture in the hallway was mad, mad like a cartoon character with smoke coming out of her ears. Bring her into it! She was already in it. Always had been, always would be. How dumb could they get? She got up and ran into the kitchen, not bothering to soften her footsteps. If they heard, it was just too bad.

The refrigerator breathed its cold breath on her like a sea monster. She felt it through her pajamas and listened to the machine's familiar hum. She sat on the counter drinking cool milk out of a kitchen glass and slurping the way she wasn't supposed to in public.

The red kitchen clock said ten minutes after eleven.

She watched the second hand go around. The clock had its own electrical noise that was different from the refrigerator's. Every time the second hand went past four it made a tiny grinding growl you could only hear when everything else was quiet. "Grrr," said the clock now. "I'm stuck here on the wall waving my hands in circles. If only I could get down I'm sure I could do something exciting. I wish I were an egg-beater or a meat-grinder. Here comes that four again. Grrr."

It was an old game Janie had played before. The stove, she knew, wished it were a volcano, the humble teaspoons wished they were steamshovels, and the sink wished it were a wishing well so all the others could have their wishes. Yet they all stayed exactly the same, no matter what they wished, no matter what they saw and heard.

She sat there on the counter for quite a while after her milk was finished, but she supposed she'd have to go back to bed sometime. When she returned to her own room she could still hear voices, although the light was out and the words were muffled. She lay on her stomach and pushed her ear into the pillow, but it was no good. When she wriggled the springs creaked with her weight. They would keep on creaking, she found, if you sort of rocked yourself back and forth on the mattress. Hrunk hrunk, hrunk hrunk. It was a soothing noise, like Gram's old porch swing. She burrowed herself into the noise until she was really asleep.

5

On West 116th Street it went on being summer no matter what. People walked their dogs, the Mister Softee truck came around, the sprinklers were turned on in the playgrounds, and conversations were held on front steps or through open windows. Sometimes it was warm and sometimes it was warmer. It stayed light late and there were more old men who slept in doorways, more people selling things from pushcarts, more noise of radios, and lots more smells in the street—from pizza, gasoline, dry-cleaning fumes, and dog manure to an occasional whiff of river water. In short, the world went on just as if nothing had happened, and the crazy thing was that in some ways it seemed as if nothing had. Nobody said a word about what had happened that Friday evening and her parents went right on working in the library, calling clients, and drawing sketches as uninterruptedly as the hands on the kitchen clock.

For a couple of days Janie felt bad about having listened to the argument. Eavesdropping was on the list of things that weren't polite. But there had been other times when it was impossible *not* to hear. Of course, she supposed, a really polite person would have turned on the radio or gone in the bathroom and run the water. But Janie Harris simply wasn't that much of a goody-goody.

Whenever she could, these days, she spent time outside the apartment. That was why she was hanging around the public library on 114th Street the day she found out about the lecture.

The library was one large, high-ceilinged room, not as big as the school assembly hall, but much bigger than any of the classrooms. The walls were a worn-out brown, the floors were scuffed, and the lights were ugly fluorescent trays with square things like ice dividers in them. There was nothing on the floor of the library except a few long tables with chairs that didn't quite match each other, and of course the rows and rows of bookshelves that ran down the middle of the room like lengths of free-standing wall. The molded metal plates on the ceiling were coming loose, there was wire netting over the high windows to keep out pigeons and burglars, and the four big electric fans that whirred all day in the corners were furry with soot. But even though it was about the most *un*decorated place she had ever seen,

Janie liked the library. She could never understand why people made jokes about libraries being so dull and quiet. This one wasn't. Even on a summer weekday there was a constant stream of people coming in through the big double doors that were propped open on account of the heat. Women with shopping bags came in and went right over to the corner where the "Pay Duplicate" collection was kept—the best-sellers in bright jackets that cost ten cents a day to read. Little kids came scuttling through on their way to the children's section upstairs, teenagers clustered around the record collection, and there were always several elderly people reading the Spanish and Hebrew newspapers in the magazine corner. Today Janie particularly noticed a girl who looked a bit like Barbara-from-Barnard. She was sitting on the floor near the reference shelf reading the fourth volume of the *Encyclopaedia Britannica*. Other book borrowers climbed over her or reached around her, but she paid no attention. She looked as if she had finished volumes one, two, and three, and was trying to make it through volume four before dinner. Janie wondered whether the girl was reading about the Class Struggle. As usual, she was also keeping an eye out for Mrs. Karanda.

She had begun to wonder where Mrs. Karanda could be, because Mrs. Karanda was the librarian and the librarian was always supposed to be there. Mrs. Karanda was one of the things that made the library special to Janie. She was a tall black woman who walked between the stacks as if she knew every single book on every shelf—not only its title, author, and number, but also its secret meaning and who had borrowed it last. Mrs. Karanda was wonderful to look at, and nice, too. (That surprised Janie a little because so many good-looking people were stuck-up and a pain to have around.) Mrs. Karanda was different. She didn't mind if people sat on the floor to read or if kids came in and used the grown-up library the way Janie was doing.

Naturally, there were other people who worked in the library besides Mrs. Karanda, but none of them was like her and none was the librarian. It was something special to be the librarian, Janie had observed. It meant knowing where everything was and helping people find out how many chickens lived in China or how to fix a broken sewing machine. As far as Janie could see, Mrs. Karanda always did help them, without flapping or fussing. Most of all, she was always there in the midst of all the changing faces. Like your favorite book, you could go back to her again and again and she would not have changed at all.

Now Janie saw Mrs. Karanda and one of the other library people coming out of the little office that was partitioned off in one corner. They headed right toward the place where Janie was sitting, on her private perch, a useless little wedge of a shelf stuck between the end of one bookcase and the wall. Between her and the door was a shallow, glass-fronted cabinet where the two women stopped. They must be going to change the display in the cabinet, since they were carrying between them a big piece of colored paper, a number of clippings, and some thumbtacks. Everything would have been fine if a very old gentleman wearing a long overcoat (in June!) hadn't come slowly through the door with a copy of the *Daily News* held up in front of him. He bumped hard into Mrs. Karanda, who stumbled and let go of her end of the big paper in order to steady the old gentleman. He seemed as much startled by the sudden whirl of papers around him as by the collision.

For a minute it looked like a dance with autumn leaves. Then Janie slipped off her shelf and began helping to pick up the papers while everyone apologized to everyone else in Spanish and English.

And there was Janie with a collection of clippings in her hands, feeling foolish suddenly because Mrs. Karanda didn't know her and would probably think it was very dumb that there was a person who spent so much time watching her and comparing her to books and so on.

But Mrs. Karanda wasn't going to stand around while anyone was feeling foolish. She swept up the last pieces of paper and handed them to her assistant, whom she called Angie, neatly intercepted a woman with a stroller before she could run over the thumbtacks, and asked Janie to open the cabinet for her, all more or less in one motion. "Well, thank you very much for rescuing us. I must have looked pretty funny there for a minute, waltzing all over the landscape." She laughed and took the first of the clippings from Janie. "I know you. You're the one who always sits on that little shelf reading the big sculpture books. It's many long years since I was any way narrow enough to sit there, but it's a good place for those who fit. Maybe you'd like to help Miss Warnick and me set up the new bulletin board."

Without making Janie answer, Mrs. Karanda, with Miss Warnick to help her, was pulling down the old display, a collection of cookbook jackets, an announcement about cooking classes being given by a Chinese woman, and a chart showing what vitamins a person ought to eat every day. The new display, as it began to take shape, was much more interesting. First there was bright turquoise paper for the background and then a very neatly lettered sign saying, "Summer in Old New York: Community Evenings at the Morningside Heights Library." That went across the top. Then again there were some new book jackets. The books were all about New York in some way—a novel about the times of Peter Stuyvesant, a guide to "New York's Smaller Museums," and a book about wildlife in Central Park. Right in the middle was a printed leaflet headed, "Third Season! Summer Library Talks—Topics of Local Interest—Free—Tuesday Evenings at 7."

"Are you going to come to our program on Tuesday?" asked Mrs. Karanda as Janie handed her a tack. "There's going to be a lecture with slides about the carved statues and decorations on New York buildings. That ought to be right down your alley."

Janie was doubtful. "I don't know," she said, "isn't it supposed to be just for grownups?" She had an uncomfortable picture of herself completely surrounded by terribly tall people, all squeezed and tripped over and stared at because she was the only kid in the room.

But Mrs. Karanda was definite. "Oh, no. These talks are for everybody. Of course, I don't want to kid you. It *is* mostly old types like me and Angie who come, but there are always some young ones too. Don't you see where it says 'Community' there?"

Actually, Janie wasn't a bit sure kids *were* part of the community, according to most people. But if Mrs. Karanda thought differently that was fine with Janie Harris. "Okay," she said, grinning. "It sounds cool. I'll come. That is, I'll have to ask my parents, but they'll probably say yes. I mean, I hope they will."

"Well, that's just fine. Maybe your parents would like to come along. Everyone welcome. Don't forget, now, Tuesday at seven." Mrs. Karanda was gathering up the old bulletin board stuff and heading back to the office. She turned and looked at Janie, really looking at her like a complete, noticeable person. "If sculpture's your thing, I know you'll find those slides very interesting. And thanks again for helping."

"Oh, thank *you*. I'll really come." But she was talking to Mrs. Karanda's back.

Janie headed slowly back for the apartment, lingering in front of a toy store window and trying not to remember that she hadn't yet picked up the shell collection she had left scattered all over her rug.

The toy store had a Slinky in its window, one of those long, smooth metal springs you could juggle with or make go downstairs end over end. The Slinky was on a wooden platform that tipped back and forth electrically so that it poured its metal self from side to side. Janie worked into a good daydream in which she was figuring what it would be like to be a Slinky and move by flipping forward, first on your hands, then on your feet. People did that in the circus sometimes, only faster. What did Slinkies eat? Probably little bits of metal that they sucked up into their hollow middles. Then they grew longer at one end, like a seashell making its spiral—Omigosh, those shells.

Janie was off around the corner so fast that someone's stiff, gray-muzzled old boxer dog started barking after her as if she were the ghost of every delivery boy and alley cat he'd ever chased. She wasn't really late, she told herself. There wasn't any rule about when she had to be back as long as she didn't miss dinner. Just the same, she used her keys very quietly. Maybe if she went right in and picked up the shells her mother would think she'd done it that morning.

Mom's voice came from the living room as clearly as if there were six microphones in the hall. "—try so hard with this family. Sometimes I just don't know why I bother." So Dad must be home already.

Janie walked very carefully into her room, not hurrying, not dawdling, and shut the door behind her. She went over to her shell collection, put her foot on her biggest, most favored whelk shell, and crunched it into gritty bits. Then she got down on her knees and picked up all the other shells very neatly. Back they went in their Bloomingdale's box—all the clams, the jingle shells, the sand dollars, periwinkles, whelks, razor clams, and skate's egg cases. Each one had once had an animal living inside it, an animal that could crawl back in its shell if it didn't like what was going on outside. "Well, I don't care," said Janie aloud. "I don't care at all." She put the box away and went into the bathroom, making as much noise as she could, turning on the water very loud and banging the bathroom stool with her foot. The sound of voices in the living room stopped abruptly.

That night after dinner Janie took down the little picture of Sargie that hung on her wall and stared at it for a long time. It was funny that a picture should be the thing she always went to when she felt awful. Stuffed animals were nicer to hold, but Sargie was special—a very special picture just the way he'd been a very special dog.

Sargeant Pepper was his real name and he had belonged to Gram. The summer when Janie was three, an old friend of Gram's had given Gram Sargeant Pepper to keep her company, now that she'd decided to live on Dixon's Island all year round instead of going back to the apartment in Boston for the winter. Sargie was just a bouncing, hairy tennis ball of a puppy and he and Janie had "just sort of raised each other," Gram always said. It was Janie's first whole summer on the island, and together she and Sargie had learned all about everything—how to go down the steep stone steps to the water, how to climb over slippery rocks, how not to get nipped by the little pink-clawed hermit crabs, how to stay out of poison ivy, how to chase the woodchuck out of the tomatoes, how *not* to chase the bantam hens, how to reach up to the stone crock in the dark pantry where the molasses cookies lived.

That summer, and every summer after, Sargie was always right beside her, barking to let strangers know they'd better be nice to His Girl, licking yellow-jacket stings and scraped elbows ("not very sanitary," said Dad), and bringing her presents that ranged from interesting stones to very dead fish. "That's because he's French," explained Gram about the fish. "He's a gourmet like your Uncle Arthur." Sargie *was* French, an unusual kind of dog called a griffon, and pronounced "*gree*-fawn."

He really had been a wonderful dog, just about the only dog Janie had ever known ("you know, *known*, like a person"). Mom and Dad both thought it was wrong to keep a dog in the city and although Alan and Evalee had a fat old cocker spaniel, even they had to admit that Coco was about as interesting as a sofa cushion with bad breath. Coco was dead now, anyway, and Sargie was dead too. He had been run over two winters ago by somebody who was "probably in a hurry to get to the ferry" and didn't even stop. Gram kept saying she was going to get a new puppy, but somehow she didn't get around to it, and Janie thought she knew why. There wouldn't be another Sargie. All that was left of him was this portrait that Mom had painted and given to her for Christmas when she was five. Janie thought of it as her most valuable possession. When she looked at the picture she always felt Sargie was right there, still watching out for her and licking her feet and cuddling up to her when she had a stomach ache. Mom had done the portrait in watercolor, but it didn't look so thin and washy as watercolors often did, even the ones in museums. In this picture the dog's little body looked as hard and warm and real as if he had been sitting on her bed. One ear was up, the other was down, both front legs were planted defiantly, and from his underslung jaw trailed an accidental strand of seaweed. The picture always made Janie feel good just to look at it. After all, it wasn't as if she still missed the real Sargie that much. A year and a half was a long time.

The sigh she gave as she looked at the picture now was an envious one, not a sad one. She would never learn to paint the way Mom could, not in a zillion, quptillion years. By now she had even given up trying to do Sargie in clay. There was something impossible about all that long hair. Either he came out looking like nothing but hair with no shape underneath or else he looked like a dog with some hair pasted on him. She had tried it both ways so often that Mr. Snaith, her art teacher, had suggested she try dachshunds instead because they were smoother. Huh. Dachshunds!

Janie turned the picture over on its face and began wiggling at the nails that held the back in place. They were good and loose from other times when she had done the same thing. Underneath the cardboard, on the back of the picture, it said:

"Merry Christmas to Janie
from Sargie and me and Santa Claus.
All my love, Mother."

Opposite the place where it said Santa Claus there was a small red-suited Santa with glasses, who looked remarkably like Dad. Opposite "me" was a red kiss mark, and opposite "Sargie" was a paw print, a real paw print in green ink. ("He was terribly good about making the print," Mom said, "but he hated having his paw washed afterward. We both ended up covered with green.")

Janie put back the cardboard and pushed the little nails into the frame again. She hung it back on the wall, being very careful that it was safely on the hook. It was too bad she had broken her best whelk shell that day, she thought, because people ought to hold onto things they were fond of. The real thing was not to care when important things were taken away and there was nothing you could do. Not caring seemed to be one of the things that had to be learned as you got older. She was going to learn it.

6

The next day Mom took Janie to a dentist's appointment that had been put off from a time in May when she had a cold. Janie really didn't mind going to Dr. Fraser—not very much, anyway. He used a water drill, never asked her dumb questions she couldn't answer when her mouth was propped open, and had a big tank full of tropical fish for her to watch while he worked. Of course, you would probably have to be soft in the head to *love* going to the dentist, but the fish were interesting and Mom always took her to Schrafft's afterward. There, no matter what time of day it was, she would have a toasted cheese sandwich and a double-thick vanilla milkshake.

This time Janie and her mother were both pleased because Janie had no cavities. They walked around the corner to the air-conditioned restaurant and sat down at a table by the window. "Heavens, it's hot," said Mom, pushing the hair back from her face. "Janie, don't you wish we were out on the bay in the *Singing Oyster* right now?"

"Wow, do I!" The *Singing Oyster* was Gram's little sailboat that took them back and forth to town for groceries in good weather. "I wish you and Gram and Dad and I were all sailing out to the sandbar for a picnic." Janie was surprised at the question. She hadn't thought her mother missed Dixon's Island that much. There was a silence while Janie sipped at her milkshake. Her mother was resting her chin on her hands and her iced tea was untouched. Janie thought she looked happier—or was it younger?—than she had in a long time.

"A picnic," she said at last. "That would be nice. Or maybe a clambake and some of your daddy's fried chicken. And afterwards a long, long sail. Maybe right out of the bay into the ocean. Maybe all the way to Italy, or Greece, or maybe Ireland."

"What will you do when you get there?" Janie spoke quietly, not wanting to interrupt.

"Oh, look at all the pictures in the museums. Go to parties on board famous private yachts. Drink Cinzano in all the outdoor cafes. . . ."

The waitress came with their check, and Janie's mother stopped talking and began getting ready to go. "Well. That's enough daydreaming for a while. Was your sandwich good, darling? If we don't have to wait

67

too long for the bus, I can still get a little work done this afternoon."

As the bus carried them back uptown, Janie asked, "Mom, that sailing trip you were talking about—across the ocean and all. Were you going to take me and Dad and Gram? It sounded sort of as if you were alone. You weren't going to go and leave us, were you?"

"Why, darling, of course not. People talk about things they don't intend to do. You know that. How could I possibly go away and leave you without anybody to change the beds and sew on the buttons? I was just having fun pretending myself an adventure, that's all. You must learn not to find so many things to worry about." She patted Janie's hand.

"But why were you *pretending* that?"

"Oh, honey. I know it's hard for you to understand. There are things you think you have in life, sometimes, and then you find you don't have them after all. And then there are other things you think you don't need because you can always get them, and then one day the chance is gone. If you have any sense, you just go along from day to day and try not to brood about it, I suppose. I'm sorry, I guess I'm not making much sense to you. Okay?"

"Okay," echoed Janie obediently. But it wasn't hard for her to understand at all.

When they got home there was still a little time before dinner. Janie wanted to go and see Griff. Since she had found the way to get up to him, she had spent a lot of time visiting him. In some way, he was especially hers, a wonderful discovery, a friend she couldn't lose. Best of all, he was always there. She went up the now familiar green stairs.

From his pedestal, Griff seemed to be staring north. Janie thought he must be able to see beyond the maze of buildings on Manhattan, past the Cloisters and Fort Tryon, up to wherever the Hudson came from and even through Canada into the Arctic. Janie scrambled up beside him and let her mind slide out along the imagined pathway. Under her arm the stone was cool and friendly. Its solidity helped her not to look straight down at the street, which was something she really didn't want to do. She put her hand up on the carved feathers between the two pointed ears. Then she felt it, as she had half known she would.

Inside the stone, deep beneath fur and feathers, there was a slow surge. Janie waited very quietly beside the stone griffin, feeling through her hand the change that was taking place.

"Hello, Griffin," said Janie softly.

The voice that answered her was somewhat dry and gritty. "How do you do? I am glad you called me. It has been a long time."

"I wanted you to talk to me. I was sure you could. Is it all right if I get up on your back? I like it up there."

"It is all right, but be careful. I am still a little stiff."

Cautiously, she put her foot on his elbow and lifted herself into the place behind his neck. She settled back so that the two incurved wings came up behind her like a chair back, like a careful hand holding her. She looked around behind her at the wing tips where they joined above her head. In the late afternoon sun they were no longer gray stone but as bronze as the feathers of Gram's hens. The wings were golden and glowing, with a purple-brown sheen, and the vein that ran up the center of each feather was pure copper. No hen had ever had feathers like these, so long and strong and splendid. Janie turned forward again and saw the tall, slender ears twitch as the griffin felt her movement.

"Well? Do you like me, now that you've called me?"

"Yes, oh yes. You're beautiful. Even better than when you were stone."

"Stone? But I *am* stone. Yesterday, today, and to-morrow, stone. It's what I'm made of." The falcon's head turned a little and looked at her out of one dark, gleaming eye the color of an amethyst. She could hear the tiny, dry rustle of the neck feathers as he moved.

Janie felt insulted. "How can you be just stone? Anybody can see that's not so."

"Stone plus, not just stone," he corrected. "There's a world of difference, as you're going to find out."

"I am?"

"Of course. I am quite a fascinating creature," admitted the griffin, "and we are going to get to know each other very well. I can take you to places you have never seen. I can show you this city as only seagulls and steeplejacks know it. I will know your secret wishes and never laugh at them. I can listen to your most secret thoughts and never tell them. When we fly together the rivers will make rainbows over our heads and the moon will roll over like a dog asking to be petted. Have you ever gone helicopter-herding or played rooftop hopscotch? What about balloon tag? Just think of the things we can do together. If only we had more time, I would tell you. . . ." He shifted his feet and cocked an eye toward the sun.

"Tell me what?"

"Oh, many things. Tales of lost empires and the time when the myths were real. Right now, however, I have to tell you that it's getting late. You'd better be off downstairs or someone will come looking for you. And that wouldn't be good."

But Janie had already slipped down from the griffin's back. He was right; she must go. "When can I come again?" she asked.

The great creature had moved back to his statue pose, gazing straight out over the street, but one ear twitched toward her and she felt him lean up against her hand like a cat wanting to be scratched. "When it's safe, little one. When it's safe. You will know when."

Already, as Janie walked toward the stairway access, she could see that bronze feathers, polished beak, and tawny hide were hardening into gray once more. Suddenly, in the violet shadow of the parapet, she felt cold. She called across the tarred roof, "You're not going back to stone, are you? Like before?"

The reply was low and jerky, the way his voice had been when she first heard it. "To stone, yes. But not to sleep. Not all the way. I will still be here when you want me."

7

Janie carried her secret with her all evening, keeping it between her and what went on at home, planning for the next time she would be able to go up to the roof. However, the next day was rather an inside-out one, and nothing went the way she had expected. First of all, Mom suddenly decided that it was about time she and Janie got down to giving a delayed spring cleaning to Janie's room.

As always, cleaning was both boring (because there was so much of it) and exciting (because you never knew what you'd find that you had forgotten about).

"Darling, what on *earth* did you want with an entire shoebox of dried seaweed?"

Janie herself discovered three sticks of gum under the paper in her bureau drawer, a paperback copy of

Three Children and It, a winter hat of Alan's, and (hurrah) her missing Swiss Army knife. Not so nice to find were a big stain on the rug under the bed, one of the good kitchen knives (the one she had borrowed), and a lot of penicillin pills under the mattress where she had stuck them instead of taking them for her bronchitis last winter.

"Honestly, Janetta. I don't know what I'm supposed to do with you. You just don't seem to learn."

Mom was pretty mad about the knife and the pills, all right, but after all they were over and done with and the subject was finally dropped. The rug was a problem, though. Janie had been promised that she could redecorate her room in the fall, and it was part of the plan that the rug would be dyed. The spot might spoil that. As they finished up, she and Mom talked about other ideas for the redecoration.

Then suddenly it was five thirty, and five thirty on Tuesday, too. Janie remembered with a jerk that this was the day of the sculpture lecture at the library. It almost didn't seem worth asking to go, since it was so late. Dad would be home soon, it was nearly time for dinner and Mom had gone to wash and change after her "day in the hyena's den." It wasn't the best time to ask Mom for anything when she was feeling tired and grubby so Janie lay in wait for her father and slipped in between him and his evening paper. "Dad, there's this lecture thing at the library tonight at seven. . . ." That was sneaky, because she knew he'd have to answer.

"*A* lecture, not '*this* lecture thing,' babe. What's it about?"

Surprisingly, Dad was not only willing to have her go, he even offered to take her and bring her back. "Fine idea," he said. "Much better than TV. I'll come and get you at eight fifteen. Don't leave without me if it's over before then."

Why eight fifteen? Janie wanted to know. "Oh," said Dad airily, "I know these community programs. We used to have them in school—that was when I was teaching in Brooklyn. They're always planned to run an hour and they always start late, so eight fifteen should just about do it."

"Don't forget," Dad repeated, as he left her off at the library door after dinner, "I'll come and get you at eight fifteen. Got your watch?"

Janie nodded. The library doors were propped open and quite a lot of people, mostly grownups, were going inside and up the stairs to the children's library, where the lecture was going to be. They looked warm and tired, and some, who came with a husband or wife, looked as if they'd rather be somewhere else. The main way they looked was big and strange, however. Janie began to wonder whether she'd be able to find a seat she could see from and whether this was really going to be as interesting as she'd expected. "Why don't you come too?" she said, looking sideways at her father. But he only gave her shoulder a squeeze and turned away down the street. "Not tonight, Jan-Jan.

You're the stone-lover in this family. Have a good time and I'll see you later."

Janie didn't think much of the way the lecture began. The man from the Museum of the City of New York who was giving it looked as though he'd been *in* the museum for quite a while—at least since he gave his last lecture. Not that he was old or anything, in fact he was about as young as her father. But he had smooth, pinkish skin, like a doll nobody is allowed to play with, and even in the warm library he had on a suit with a matching sort of vest underneath.

At the beginning he was just talking about the history of New York and Janie squirmed around on her hard chair and wondered why the neat young doll-man didn't look as hot as anybody else. Even Mrs. Karanda, who sat in the front row wearing beautiful moon-shaped earrings and a high turban, was fanning herself with a copy of the folder describing the lectures. Janie was just beginning to count the number of things she could see in the room that began with the letter S (sweater, Scotch tape, shoes, sunburn, shelf, stool, slide projector) when she came back with a jerk to hear the museum man saying, "—of which this library itself is an excellent example. How many times have those of you who live in the neighborhood passed by without noticing the Romanesque gargoyles, that is, grotesque imaginary creatures, ornamenting the false beam ends that mark the transition from ashlar to brick in the building's second story?"

Janie had no notion what ashlar or Romanesque might

mean, but she certainly knew those gargoyles, if that was what they were called. There were four of them—little, hunched-over figures that looked like grinning old men with long noses, bat's wings, pointy ears, horns, and other features that showed they were not quite human. Each of them held something in his hands that seemed to be connected with libraries or learning. One had an old-fashioned ink bottle, one an hourglass, one a complicated instrument sort of like a globe, and one (her favorite) held a book and had his nose so far into it that he would clearly get it pinched when he shut the covers. This library, the lecturer was saying, had been built by the same famous architect who had designed some of the big buildings at Columbia and other colleges in the city. Many of the gargoyles and animals on those buildings had been carved by the same workman and his helpers. He was a man who had had a workshop in Brooklyn many years ago and had come there from Poland. Later in the program they were going to see some old photographs of that man and his workshop, but now they would look at slides of some of the "interesting and historic" carvings on old buildings, first from Morningside Heights and then from other parts of the city.

From that point on, Janie was lost. She forgot all about the hard chair and the fact that the thin woman next to her needed to use a Kleenex and hadn't brought one. She only saw the sculptured creatures on the screen. They came from churches, colleges, apartment houses, synagogues, theaters, city office buildings, department stores, hotels, museums, monuments, clubs, and even ordinary houses. Janie had been feeling a little pleased with herself because *she* had noticed the gargoyles on the library (and Griff, of course Griff), but now she understood that she'd been going around all her life looking at sidewalks while over her head and behind her back a whole zoo full of sculpture was being ignored and "subjected to indignities by pigeons," as the museum man said. He didn't seem to like pigeons, and after her day on the roof with the Lestoil, Janie understood why. She decided she liked him better.

The lecturer began pointing out that the carvings were not only wonderful by themselves but represented many different styles. The names of those—neoclassical, Gothic, art nouveau—just washed over Janie without her noticing, but the look and shape of them made her fingers twitch with wanting to try to make things that way herself. She began listening seriously again when the man started talking about the stonemasons who had made the stone carvings. They were not architects or famous artists but skilled workmen who carried on a long tradition. Apparently they were mostly men who had learned the art of stonecarving in Europe and sometimes they had a hard time finding work after they came to the United States because not so many people wanted statues for their gardens and not so many towns wanted fountains or public monuments.

The photographs of the old stonecutter were rather

worn and scratchy since they were so old, but Janie was fascinated to see the place where the big blocks of stone were brought to be carved and the handmade tools that were used to do it. They were the old-fashioned tools that had been used in Europe for centuries, so the museum man said. After the fashion for ornamented buildings died out and everything was supposed to be all smooth and "modern," most of the old craftsmen had been forced to retire or find other jobs. Now almost nobody did that kind of work anymore. The last few pictures showed the old man working. The lecturer read a quotation from him concerning the different kinds of stone for carving—Vermont granite, Iowa limestone, Italian marble. He touched the big blocks and spoke about them as if they were alive.

That was the end of the lecture. Janie clapped as hard as she could until she noticed that most of the rest of the audience was applauding much more calmly and politely. She stopped abruptly, wondering whether her face were as red as it felt, and got up to join the departing crowd. At the front of the room Mrs. Karanda and two or three other people were talking to the museum man. Over his shoulder the librarian caught Janie's eye and smiled as if to say, "Come and join us." Janie would have liked to thank Mrs. Karanda for inviting her to the lecture, but she really didn't feel like talking just then. Behind her eyes filed a procession of eagles holding arrows, lions guarding shields, unicorns, hounds, dragons, rams, and naked people out of mythology. She almost missed her father, who was waiting for her on the steps outside. "Hey," said a voice above her left ear, "there goes my daughter. Stop that girl. Jan-Jan, have you disowned me?"

"Huh? Oh, hi Dad. No, I was just thinking."

Together they turned and headed for Riverside Drive. "Good show?" he asked.

"Yeah, great." Still walking, but backwards, she turned around to take a farewell look at the gargoyles. Other people were doing the same thing, so that the sidewalk in front of the library was clustered with up-turned faces like dim balloons. The gargoyles peered down in the fading light as if delighted with the sudden attention. "Great," she repeated, "real great," and for once her father didn't make her change "real" to "really."

It had turned into one of those New York summer evenings when everything seemed to have come to a gentle halt. Usually that only happened in a snowstorm, but now it was as if the sunset sky had snowed pink silence down into the streets, filling them from top to bottom. Even the traffic on the West Side Highway sounded distant and the only movement on the Hudson was a small sailboat far off toward the Palisades side. Groups of passersby talked quietly. When a single late seagull glided low over the Drive like a paper airplane she could plainly hear its harsh but homelike squawk. She had taken Dad's hand and they walked along comfortably without needing to talk.

Janie kept one eye on the buildings they were passing. Most of them just had brick fronts or geometric designs on them, but when the two strollers came to a big old apartment house with a half-moon driveway curving in toward its entrance, there by the doorway stood a small and very gentle-looking stone lion with ringlets in his mane and an iron lamp post clasped in his paws. "Lyon Court" was written in big letters on the building's front, which Janie supposed was why somebody had thought it would be nice to put a lion there. It was a perfect end to the day.

They went up in the elevator, which happened miraculously to be waiting for them. Janie opened the apartment door because she got her key from around her neck before Dad could get his out of his trousers pocket. It was a game they played.

Dad headed toward the bedroom and Janie turned down the hall to the kitchen because she wanted a popsicle.

"*Janetta Harris, where have you been?* Don't you know it's almost nine o'clock?"

Janie felt as if she'd already had the popsicle— swallowed it down whole and frozen, stick and all. She searched her mind frantically but there was no mistake. "Mom, it was just that lecture. I told you, remember? At dinner. Dad was right there. He said he'd come and pick me up afterwards and he did."

"I don't care what you told me at dinner. *Nobody, ever*, gave you permission to be out this late, young lady."

"But—but Dad said—he said he'd wait." She was trying so hard not to cry that she had to keep tight hold of every breath or it would run away and turn into a sob.

"Don't give me any more buts. I have had it, really had it with your excuses. I don't care what you've been doing all this time, or your father either. I don't want to hear about it. Now go to your room."

But Janie couldn't. Behind her was nothing but the kitchen door and her mother seemed to fill the hallway in front of her, like a police roadblock with sirens and flashing red lights. Janie read on her mother's face not only anger, but confusion and hurt. What she had done must be really terrible, but Janie didn't understand why, and she knew she wouldn't find out. Her mother's eyes were focused on the air, almost as if it weren't really Janie she was seeing. Abruptly, Mary Harris pressed the heels of her hands over her eyes, then turned and walked back down the hall without a word.

Janie stood staring at the leaves on the wallpaper, three of which made a down-curved beak and two up-right ears. Suddenly she was boiling mad. She hadn't done anything, not anything she wasn't supposed to do. It was Dad who had said eight fifteen, but he'd also said he'd wait for her. Nobody'd ever suggested she was supposed to leave before the program was over. Besides, nine wasn't all that late; in summer she was usually allowed to stay up till nine thirty. How was she supposed to know she'd get into trouble like that? It wasn't fair, not fair at all, and things *ought* to be fair. Dad

was always telling her, "Jan-Jan, in this world there are a lot of things that aren't the way they ought to be. You have to live with it like anybody else." But that was for things like catching measles at Christmas or students getting shot at peace demonstrations—not for the way your own family acted.

By now Janie had pushed down the first red-hot part of her anger. She was about to go to her room as she'd been told when she heard her father come out of the bathroom and into the living room. Mom must have been sitting there waiting for him. "I suppose it won't do me any good to ask where you've been for two hours."

When he answered, Dad sounded merely exasperated. "Oh, for God's sake, Molly, where do you think I was? Getting drunk in a cheap saloon? I took Janie to the library and then I went for a walk, that's all. It was a nice evening. *Was*. You're certainly not making me sorry I missed those two hours of domestic tranquillity."

Janie's bedroom door closed behind her smoothly. Facing each other in front of the stereo cabinet, her parents had never noticed the sneaker-footed shadow that dived across the front hall to safety.

Janie got ready for bed and decided not to take a bath or brush her teeth. If she were going to be scolded anyway, she might as well be really bad. Besides, she would have had to open her door and cross the hall to the bathroom, and she didn't want to do that.

She got out a lump of plasti-clay and began molding

and mushing it around absentmindedly. It was old and stiff and she had to pound it on the desk top to get it soft again. After a while she sat on the bed with her arms on the windowsill just watching the cars and people on the street. But every time she stopped to look at what her hands were doing she found herself making an animal that was half lion and half falcon. Finally she got into bed, thinking about the stone griffin—"stone plus"—who stood on the roof in the nighttime glow of the city. Griffins were supposed to guard things. Or people. She hoped that was what this one was doing.

8

Janie could have gone up to the roof right after breakfast the next morning. Certainly that was what she had intended to do when she got up. Instead, she was surprised to find herself messing around in her room—unmessing, really—doing a bunch of little things that were leftover from the big clean-up yesterday. She went through a stack of old letters, school papers, valentines, and so on, deciding which ones to keep and which to throw away. She tried on a pile of last year's clothes to see which ones were really too small for her. She began untangling the strings of a clown marionette that Uncle Arthur had brought her from Holland.

The strings were really snarled around each other, but Janie worked patiently. She was being *good*, she knew—doing things Mom would approve of, even though she wasn't at all sure she cared what Mom thought.

It had been very late last night when the bedroom door opened and let the light in from the hall. Mom always came to kiss her if she hadn't said good night before, of course, but this time Janie felt she had been asleep a long time when the usual sounds came. They were like having someone else walking in your sleep, these nighttime visits, and sometimes Janie was so deep asleep in the cave of her own body that she hardly did more than give a contented wriggle at the feel of the weight on the bed and the familiar words, "Goodnight, darling. Mother loves." This time, however, she came to the cave mouth quickly and when she made slits of her eyes against the hall light she saw her mother sitting very straight on the edge of the bed with her face half lit, like a mask for a play.

"Darling, are you awake?"

Janie said nothing, but opened her eyes wider and made a half-asleep noise in her throat. Mom had had a hand on her arm. Now she took it away and sat looking at her fingers as if she wondered what they would do next. "Darling, Janie. I shouldn't have been so mad with you this evening. I'm sorry. I was—upset about something. I didn't. . . ." She stopped for a minute. "I mean, is it all right again? People do these things."

Lying still in her warm cave of sleep and silence, Janie felt two different answers jam in her mouth, fighting to get out like passengers leaving a subway car.

"Yes," cried one of them, "oh yes, it's all right. You could never do anything to make me mad forever." "No!" bellowed the other one. "You hurt me and why should I say what you want? No, no, no!" But already the unspoken argument was over.

"Sure, Mom, it's okay. G'night." She felt her mother's kiss on her cheek and for a moment she pressed back hard. Then she rolled on her side as if to avoid the light, and burrowed back into her cave. As she fell asleep again, hugging her knees and hearing the door close, she knew she had lied. The answer had been no all the time.

Yet here she was the next day, being good, while Mom was working in her office and Griff was waiting up on the roof. As she thought that thought, Janie realized why she was lingering so. Griff might *not* be waiting, or rather he might not be waiting to come alive for her the way he had yesterday. It might not work again. As long as she didn't go up and find out, she could hold onto the idea. It was something to look forward to. "And I have to have something," said Janie in her head. "I just have to."

It was after lunch before she started up the long green stairs. Mom had gone out and the building was quiet. Janie felt as if she were a spy creeping to a secret meeting. She moved so quietly that no electric eye could detect her or the most sensitive booby trap react to her passing. It was a good game and when, just as she reached the sixth floor landing, an elderly gentleman stuck his head out the door of 5A and peered up and down the stairwell, Janie didn't know which was better, the way her heart pounded as she froze back into the shadows, or the giggle she had to stop with her hands. The old man looked as cautious as she was. Could he be a spy too, a real one, terrified that the enemy might steal his microfilms? "Don't worry, old man. I won't tell. I have a secret too." Suddenly she felt very light and confident. Everything was fine and Griff would be waiting. She climbed the last flight of stairs and pushed open the door onto the bright roof.

The stone griffin was standing on his pedestal as usual, which made her realize she had half expected to see him sunning himself, preening his feathers, or talking to a passing pigeon. She paused at the foot of the pedestal, remembering how impossibly high it had once appeared. Slightly out of breath, she stood up beside Griff and dusted herself off. "Hey, I'm here. Did you see me coming?" Already she could see the change taking place as it had before—a sheen coming over the stone as it went from gritty gray to tawny hide and burnished feathers.

"I heard," said the griffin. "I can't see behind me any more than you can." Janie noticed that the soft feathers under his throat swelled in and out when he spoke but that his beak hardly moved. He pressed himself against her hand with a motion like a cat. "I'm glad you could get away. I thought you were missing me."

"Well, I was. It's nicer up here."

"By the way," said the griffin, "do you think I could ask you to scratch behind my right ear? It's been itching for about four years now, especially in warm weather."

"Of course," said Janie, reaching up to the ear. "I mean, I'd be glad to. Couldn't you scratch it yourself, though?" The griffin turned his head about two inches, just enough so he could look at her out of one dark eye.

"My dear friend, I can see we are going to have to have a long talk. How do you think it would look from the street if I should suddenly go down on my haunches and get after that ear with a hind foot? You seem to be quite young for a human being, so I will tell you that the effect would not be good at all. Traffic accidents, just for a start. Fire engines, helicopters. Commissions of inquiry. And worse, much worse. Besides which, there is a certain public tradition to be kept up, you know, especially for us griffins, who guard things."

"You mean like those men with red uniforms and fur hats who stand guard where the Queen lives in England and aren't allowed to move?" suggested Janie. "I saw them in a movie once. I know lots of things," she added, remembering his earlier remark, "and I'm not so young, either."

"I'm sorry," said the griffin instantly. "You have to understand that I haven't known many people. We get so little time awake these days, so very little. And the top of a building is a rather lonesome place. It's not like being on a fountain, in a plaza, or even over a doorway. Of course, the view is splendid and one can learn a lot by just watching, but there isn't much conversation, if you see what I mean. An occasional workman comes along—repairing things or putting up TV antennas. (Nice people but very blind about stonework, most of them.) And then there are always the building custodian and just a few children, like you and your friend that used to come up here two or three years ago. But there again, that's what I meant about your being young, though I'm sorry if I offended you. The two of you were interested in nothing but those foolish sparrows. I suppose it takes a certain amount of experience to appreciate the really important things. Don't stop scratching, will you? An itch as old as that needs pretty thorough attention."

Obligingly, Janie went back to work. She felt as if her mind were like the griffin's ear, itchy with questions. "Did you really know about Evalee and me when we played up here, years ago? Why didn't you talk to us then? And who is we, I mean who *are* we? I mean I know who we are (you and I). But who do you mean when you say *we?* Are there other stone animals like you?"

"My dear Miss Harris," began the griffin, "or shall I call you by your first name? I know customs have changed since the time I was carved."

He seemed to be waiting for an answer, so Janie said rather uncertainly, "Oh, I don't think you could possibly call me Miss Harris. Nobody *ever* does that, except old Mr. Snaith at the art school and Mom says he's terribly stuffy."

"In that case, then, I shall call you Janetta."

"Oh, please, not Janetta. That's not even a real name. My mother made it up because she wanted to name me after Gram but she thought Jane was too dull. She says *she* always hated being Mary and wanted something distinctive. But I like being Janie and even Mom calls me that, except when she's mad at me."

"Well then, let it be Janie. And you may call me by the name you made up years ago. Griff suits me very well. But now let me try to answer some of your questions."

He paused, and Janie could see that his eyes were fixed on the street below. The end of his tail twitched impatiently, the way a cat's does when it sees a string being trailed in front of it. The thick-muscled lion's legs began to flex and the sensitive tips of his ears trembled and swiveled around to catch the summer wind. Then she felt him heave a sigh and straighten himself. "Ah me," he said. "I know that I may seem old to you, but as stone goes—as stone goes, I am fresh from the chisel and it is very hard not to leap and soar when there is the chance. Nevertheless, 'Stone is patient.' That's our motto and I must abide by it. If I were one of my ancestors, now, those who guarded the palace gates of Persepolis or stood on the shields of Scythia, or even one of my cousins from the mighty cathedrals, I would have patience to spare. But as it is . . .

"To begin with, there are certainly more of us. That is, I suppose I mean two things when I say *we*. First, I

91

mean the rest of us griffins. We are a very ancient family, as you may know, but now is not the time to go into family history, which is almost five thousand years long. Besides the griffins, however, I also mean all the Stonefolk, at least all the quick ones. Now, I suppose, you're going to ask me which ones are the quick ones like me, and I wish I could tell you. All I *am* sure of is that we are not like you human beings. You have a certain span of life and at the end of it you gradually withdraw from life and do something called dying. For us, however, life only grows as time goes on. The older we are, the more we are quick, as we say. You will see why this should be so after you know more about us. But that is not all there is to it. Our saying, 'Stone is patient,' means, among many other things, that we become more quick as we grow older. But our other saying is 'Quickness is a gift.' The truth is that some never become quick, no matter how long they wait, while others are quick almost before they are finished."

"Yes," interrupted Janie, "but what *makes* them quick? I mean in the beginning."

Griff twitched his ears and allowed himself to turn a little left so he could gaze over the river. "There's a hawk there above the Palisades," he remarked, "one of my half cousins, you might say. Can you see him?"

"No," said Janie, squinting, "I don't think I can. I don't even see any seagulls just now. You must be able to see awfully far. But then," she added, "falcons are supposed to see far."

"Are they really?" asked Griff, sounding pleased. For a few minutes Janie thought he wasn't going to answer her original question, or perhaps had forgotten it as his eyes hovered with the distant hawk. At last, however, he said in a faraway voice, "What makes us quick? I can't really tell you. Perhaps some of the Elders know the answer, but there aren't many of them in this city, where everything is so new. And we spend so much time asleep nowadays. You don't know how good it is to be able to move and speak again after such a long time. And soon to be flying—aah. Speaking of time," he went on in a different voice, "I think it's time for you to go. If you still wonder what would happen if we were found, I suggest you take my word for it. Suppose your father came looking for you the way he did the other evening."

Janie, however, was in no doubt about the fact that Griff was *her* secret. And it *was* getting late again, especially since Mom had asked her to set the table and help hull the strawberries because some people were coming for dinner. She started to unfold herself from her seat on Griff's back, but there was one question that couldn't wait. "Griff, can you really fly?"

The griffin clattered his beak irritatedly. "My dear young lady! You might as well ask if a mermaid can swim. Do you think I have these wings for decoration?" Janie could see he was having a hard time to keep from flapping his wings as proof, but she was too excited to stop for apologies.

"Well, if you can fly, can I fly with you? On your back?"

Griff cocked an eye at her. "You could, I suppose. Yes, I think you could. But I don't know when it has been done before. It's certainly not customary. I think there are some things you would have to learn first."

"I know. You're going to say we have to be careful not to be seen. But what if—what if I came at night? No one would notice if it was dark. Shall I sneak out to-night? Shall I?"

Already Griff was going back to stone. His voice was hard and gritty, but still quite clear. "Tonight, yes. I'll be waiting. Stone is patient."

9

Janie slid through the evening like a fish through a wave. Even at the best of times she thought the Lorings, the friends of her parents who were coming to dinner, could pretty well be awarded a B+ for Boredom. Not that they had nothing to say, but the Lorings were the kind of grownups who could sit right at the table with a kid and act as if she were one of the candlesticks. The conversation might be about something she, Janie was interested in, like the new public swimming pool or a movie she had seen or somebody's trip to Japan, but the Lorings never asked her what she thought or listened when she said things. And the worst of it was that when the Lorings came her own parents seemed to catch the disease.

The Lorings had a four-year-old kid named Peter

who had some interesting thing wrong with him because he almost never talked, although when the psychologists gave him tests he always turned out to be very smart. Whenever the Lorings came, there were new stories about the specialists and doctors and clinics they had been to with Peter. It was Janie's private opinion that Peter probably didn't talk because nobody ever said any more to him than good morning and goodnight. She bet that if Peter Loring were as smart as they said he was, one day he would open up his mouth and start telling his parents that you didn't have to be twenty-one to be part of the human race.

All this was in the back of her mind as she sat at the dinner table putting more and more sugar on her strawberries and feeling, really, very much like a candlestick, or rather a candle that was slowly dripping away in the heat. And like one of the candles, nobody would notice her until she went out. In the heart of the flame of the real candle in front of her, there grew a small, purple eye that winked at her to remind her of a dark rooftop and two tall wings. Anyway, she didn't mind so much this time. She had a lot to think about.

Going up to see Griff that night wasn't going to be easy, but it shouldn't be impossible either. She would just have to be sure that she had kissed her parents so they wouldn't come in to see her before they went to bed. Then she would have to wait for the party to be over. She would have to be as patient as stone.

There. Her mother had put her napkin on the table

and everybody was getting up. Now she was allowed to say goodnight and go to her own room. Janie heard her voice saying nice, polite things. The Lorings turned and smiled at her. "Goodnight," they said, and before she was halfway to the door they were back talking about who was going to be the next mayor. That made three words they had said to her since they came, when they had both said, "Hello, there." Well, to be fair, it was six words—three each.

On her way to her room, Janie wondered briefly why she hadn't tipped over the cream pitcher, staged a choking fit, set fire to the tablecloth. At least when the Harris family was alone together nobody was supposed to be seen and not heard. For a minute Janie felt bad about her plan to sneak out. Mom and Dad were sure to worry if they missed her (and be mad, too). And dinner had been so ordinary, so cheerful and calm and pleasant (even the dumb old Lorings) that maybe everything was going to be all right after all.

Nevertheless, Janie knew she couldn't miss this adventure—not when she had made Griff come alive all by herself, and especially not when she was going to get out into the middle of the great, black, secret night. That was one of the things she loved most about Dixon's Island—the times she had been allowed to stay up late for Fourth of July fireworks or for the annual Firemen's Fair. Then there were the nights when Dad would come and wake her up so she could walk with him down the steep stony steps to the dock to see the little lights that sometimes came in the water where the waves broke. Phosphorescence, it was called. Mom didn't like going down the steps in the dark and anyway she'd seen the lights in the water a million times. But Dad had grown up near Cincinnati and never even saw a wave until he came east to college. Sometimes on those nights he would tell her about the millions of tiny creatures that lived in the water and gave off the light, but mostly they would just sit silent, watching the water, while the whole feeling of the night built itself up around them out of insect sounds, tiny rustlings or splashes, salt sea smell, sea wind, and the big wet stars overhead.

Janie loved the night, but you never got a chance to see it properly in the city. Usually you were supposed to be in bed, and when you did go out after dark it was always in a hurry to catch a bus or taxi. Being alone in the dark was dangerous and absolutely nobody took walks in it, not even grownups. A roof, now, would be different—too high up for direct street lights, and surely even more deserted than in the daytime.

By the time Janie got out of the bathtub she had it all planned. She would have to do everything the same way she always did, including putting on pajamas. Just under the edge of the bed would go the flashlight. Her clothes would go on a hook on the closet door with her sneakers underneath, ready to put on in the dark. She wasn't at all worried about getting out the front door, just about how long she would have to wait for her parents to go to bed. If only the Lorings didn't stay too late. It didn't look as if they were going to go home early, she had to admit. When she came down the hall from the bathroom she had heard that they were still discussing the election.

But now, Janie told herself, it was time to go to sleep. She turned on her side and began remembering the time, two years ago, when she and Evalee had wanted to give a surprise birthday party for Alan. Evalee had gotten a cold so she, Janie, had had to do all the actual work herself. They'd had the party at her house and Alan had been so very surprised that he got sick on the rug. Poor Alan had the kind of stomach that did that when he was excited. But he'd felt better right away and had a "super-fantastic" time. For Janie, though, the best part of the party had been afterwards when Alan and Evalee's mother and some of the parents of the other guests had come to pick up their children. The grownups were all standing around saying what a great party it had been and what a complete surprise. Evalee had ended the conversation by explaining, "It was really Janie who organized the whole thing. If she isn't going to be the world's greatest sculptor she's going to be a general." Good old Evalee. She really was loyal, in spite of running off to her cousin's. Wonder what she's doing now, out there in Wisconsin. Sleeping, dopey. . . .

When Janie woke up it felt pretty late. The slow pace of the traffic and the silence of the streets told her the early part of the night was over. She groped for her watch, buckled around the bedpost, and discovered it was ten to twelve. Moving carefully, she got out of bed and went to the door. But even before she inched the door open she could hear voices from the living room. For heaven's sake, those Lorings were still there. What about little Peter the nontalker, who must be crying in his crib because his mean parents were never coming home?

The hall was dimly lit by the light from the bathroom. Janie didn't even bother to tiptoe as she walked down to the far end and listened briefly. If anyone asked her what she was doing she was just going to the bathroom, after all. But no one gave any sign of hearing her. They were talking now about the United Federation of Teachers. Mrs. Loring was a teacher like Dad, Janie remembered. It sounded as if they were going over every single thing the union had done in the last five years. It was then that Janie decided she would just go on up and see Griff anyway. Nobody would be coming into her room that night and it was impossible to see the front hall from the end of the living room where the grownups were sitting. It would be very tricky, but she *thought* she could get out the door without being caught.

In half a minute she had skinned into her jeans, sneakers, and shirt. She closed her door behind her, slipped to the end of the hall on cautious rubber soles, and inched one eye around the corner into the living room. To her left, about ten feet away, was the front door, to her right was the open end of the living room where the stereo stood. Suddenly she froze. Suppose somebody decided to put on a record while she was opening the front door? "Janie, what are you doing?" "I guess I must be sleepwalking." "Do you always get dressed before you walk in your sleep?" No, that wouldn't be cool at all.

She actually walked backward to the front door because she had such a strong feeling that she was being watched—not just by Mom and Dad but maybe by all her teachers and several policemen as well. Then her heel hit the wall and she had to turn around to open the door. First the regular knob, then the little knob on the top lock. Pull. Then let both knobs turn back, *very* carefully. Now from the outside, close the door so slowly that there was no click—well, almost none. She was out.

As quickly and silently as rainwater, she trickled down the hallway, past the elevator and the mail chute, and through the fire door to the service stairs. The building sounded blank and echoing at this hour but Janie paid no attention. She had done it, she had gotten out in spite of everything. Nobody could keep *her* in. She was invisible. The stairs disappeared under her racing feet and here she was at the door to the roof.

The key went in upside down the first time but then she got it right and the heavy door swung open. The roof was dark but not pitch black. It is never completely dark in New York. There are too many street lights, spot lights, beacons, lighted signs, and lighted buildings. Janie could see the familiar skyline across the street, silhouetted against a navy blue sky too overcast for stars. The only really black thing was the shining path of the Hudson with the George Washington Bridge strung across it like a follow-the-dots picture made out of lights. And even blacker than the river was Griff, standing at attention on his pedestal. She called hello softly as she ran toward him.

Climbing up to Griff in the dark was not nearly as easy as it had been in daylight. It wasn't simply that she couldn't see, it was that all the spaces below her seemed much closer and deeper than before—almost bottomless. Urrrg. She stood on the board across the gap between buildings, her feet very close together, her arms hugging the cool stone corner of the pedestal. She groped for the rope, found it, and froze. No good telling herself it wasn't very far. No good remembering that she'd done this a dozen times before. She wasn't going to jump for that high place with only a piece of rope to hold onto. What if it was almost worn through in one place? She wouldn't be able to see it. She closed her eyes and seemed to feel the world tipping dangerously beneath her.

Where was Griff? Why didn't he help her?

She opened her eyes and everything tipped back with a rush. Once more the building rested on solid rock instead of Jell-O. *Quick, before everything goes all side-*

*ways again. Quick, before you get even scareder. Quick,
or you'll never find out about flying.* With no grace at
all, she scratched and heaved herself up into the dark.
Shivering, she lay for a while with her arms around one
of the lion legs. Then she felt the foot swivel in her
grasp and something furred, heavy, and prickly against
her face. Griff had turned around and was touching her
with his paw.

He took his paw away and sat down, cocking his head
birdlike so that he could see her properly. "You were
frightened," he said. "But it's only darkness, you know.
My lion half, at least, tells me that night is the finest
and freest time of all."

Janie got up a little shakily, one hand on Griff's
shoulder. In the darkness he seemed even bigger and
more solid than before. "But I like the dark. I mean, I
always have. I don't know what happened. I'm sure
I wouldn't be scared if I were up on your back. You
wouldn't let me fall off." But. . . . There was that
terribly long drop to the street. She could hear it, hear
the sound coming directly up at her. And she could
feel the drop in the top of her head and the empty part
of her stomach. There was a draft of air coming up at
her from the street—a little draft that meant empty
space where there ought to be solid ground.

Janie sat herself down on the side of the pedestal, well
back from the street. With the roof safely in front of
her, she let her feet hang over the edge, put her
elbows on her knees, plonked her chin into her hands,

and stared gloomily ahead. "I just don't get it. The other week I was standing there looking over the edge of the roof and everything was fine. I was pretending I was this fish and the street was all full of water and I was swimming down from here to Columbus Avenue. It was fun. I wasn't scared then. Is this some sort of disease you can catch?"

Griff was preening his feathers but his answer sounded as clear as ever. "Oh, I don't think it's as bad as that. You'll get over it, I'm sure. Perhaps I ought to give you flying lessons." He tensed himself and sprang down onto the roof. With wings half folded, he made a long curving glide, landing flat and smoothly half-way toward the stairs. "Come on down," he called over his shoulder. "Time enough to talk about that later. This is my first night out in thirty years."

In three bounds he was back at the foot of the pedestal, arching his great golden back like a kitten. He crouched and lashed his tail, then leaped at her as she hopped down from the crate. Janie found she had been rolled on her back as deftly as if she had been a toy mouse. The big paws batted her softly back and forth while Griff's beak, which looked as dangerous as a huge can-opener, came down to tickle her ribs deli-cately. It was incredible; it was unbearable; she was going to come apart from laughing. Panting and whoop-ing, she wriggled free and dodged behind him. The lashing tail flew at her and she grabbed it as much in self-defense as by intention. Marvelous. The griffin whirled around to catch her and Janie was swung almost off her feet in his wake. Finding her still behind him, the griffin gave a sound somewhere between a purr and a squawk and tried to swing his head around to dislodge her. Somehow his wings got in the way and all he achieved was a face full of feathers. Janie laughed so hard she let go of the tail and collapsed on her side. Mockingly, the griffin made her a bow, stretching his forelegs out in front of him.

Then he was up again and Janie found that it was she who was chasing him—over the slanting back of the stairwell, around the edge of the courtyard, up and down the part of the roof that covered the other wing. He was teasing her, keeping always half a bound ahead and stopping, when she was slow, to scratch himself, preen a feather, or gaze absentmindedly up at the sky. Once she almost caught him that way, but he leaped straight up in the air and came down six feet away with his paws already galloping. They made another whole circuit of the roof. Griff dodged around the east wing stairway access with Janie after him. Around and around they went. In Janie's head it was just like the merry-go-round at Harmonport. No matter how fast you went or how wild the music you never caught up to the rider ahead of you. But on a merry-go-round, you could only go one way. She whirled around and dashed back in the other direction. Griff met her almost face-to-beak at the low, sloping end of the stairway access. Her arms were already stretched out to tag

him but he leaped sideways onto the stairway access roof. Janie leaped with him. They raced up the slope toward the blurry summer stars and Janie caught the griffin at the very top. Gasping, she threw her arms around his neck. Griff put back his head and gave a great griffin cry of triumph and delight. It was like a gong, like a siren, like the wind in a mountain pass. Janie felt that cry rise in herself as well as in Griff, and knew then that they were truly the same creature.

The cry faded away into the larger sound of the city. The two runners sank down exhausted, the griffin with his forepaws over the edge of the roof and Janie propped slantwise against his feathered shoulder. "Oh, Griff. That was beautiful. I never—oh" (she was still out of breath) "I never heard a griffin before. I never ran so much either. Wow. But when are we going to start those lessons so I won't be afraid of falling? I've got to be able to fly with you. I've just got to."

Griff was gazing at the winking lights of a jet that was banking sharply to the west after its take-off from Kennedy Airport. "My friend Janie," he remarked to the air, "has even more to learn about patience than I do. These human beings *are* so very quick." He turned and rubbed the cool side of his beak along her face. "Don't you see, O Impatient One, that the lessons have already begun?"

Already what? Just playing on the roof? But then she began to see. "You mean I was scared to climb up on the pedestal in the dark but I wasn't scared coming down? I guess I didn't have time to think about it."

"Yes, that. And what about just now? You chased me right up to the edge, and stood there on your feet, not sitting down. That's something, even though it's not nearly as much of a drop from there to the roof as it is from the roof to the street. You'll learn, all right. It's just a question of taking things bit by bit."

"Mmmmm," said Janie comfortably, "I know." She was going to add, "Stone is patient," but somehow it didn't seem worth the trouble. Griff's shoulder was very warm and soft under her head.

"If you're going to go to sleep, little one," said his voice in her ear, "you'd better do it in your bed."

It was time to go. At the door of the stairs she turned and called softly, "G'night, Griff. And thanks." Then she was inside again. She felt exalted, magical. Instead of scaring her, the deep, late silence protected her like armor. No one would see her; she knew it. She was Janie Harris, strong and clever. One day soon she would be fearless, too, and she would fly over the dark city on wings of bronze.

She didn't even bother to keep to the shadows in the hallway, and though she did listen for a moment at the apartment door, she knew there would be nothing to hear. Working the two locks at once was tricky, but she slipped inside with hardly a sound. There was no light under her parents' door. She skinned out of her clothes in the dark and was asleep in two minutes.

IO

"What are you going to do today, darling?" asked Mom the next morning. She had come into the kitchen while Janie was finishing her breakfast—rather late because of her visit to the roof. Janie looked at her mother over her spoon with mild suspicion and took an extra long time to swallow her mouthful of cereal. Not that the question was remarkable, but recently Janie had learned to think twice before she said anything to her parents. If she were vague about her plans this time, Mom would decide she was still "moping." Then she would get another lecture about "coping." (Hey, it rhymed. *Don't mope, you gotta cope.*) Or Mom might get one of her efficient spells and decide on something (probably something dull) that would be good for her to do. She had to admit that the last time that happened it hadn't turned out too badly. Still, it would be better not to give Mom any excuse for wondering exactly what she had been doing recently.

It was then that Janie heard herself saying, "I'm going to go for a long walk, just around the neighborhood." She saw her mother start to ask where or why and added hastily, "I'm going to do some sketching." That was something she had enjoyed a lot last year, just going out in the street and drawing whatever came along, but she hadn't done it since late last fall when it got too cold to sketch. Anyway, here she was saying she was going to take up sketching again although she hadn't even thought about it until just that minute.

"Oh, really?" Mom looked approving, as Janie had been sure she would. Mom was always in favor of anything artistic, as long as it didn't make too much mess in the house. "I think that's a fine idea," her mother went on. "Just don't go too far away. And remember not to cross Broadway. I have to go to David and Dash with Mrs. Karshaw, but I'll be back around four thirty and now I'll have something to look forward to when I get home. You be sure to show me what you've done, now." She put her arm around Janie's shoulders, kissed her on the side of the head, and was gone.

Gosh, Mom was nice sometimes, Janie reflected, as she got herself another bowl of Froot Loops. She, Mom, could draw better than anybody Janie knew, even Mr. Snaith at the MacRae School (who was really a painter), but for some reason Mom didn't often like to talk about drawing or give Janie advice about it. She always said, "Oh, I'm not the one to ask. You should go to a professional." It always made Janie feel pleased when her mother would talk to her about drawing.

She began to get excited over the plan she had suddenly blurted out. She *would* sketch, but it wouldn't be dogs on leashes, boats on the river, or old people on benches. She would look for Griff's relatives, other Stonefolk like the lion with the lamp standard she had seen the other evening. She wished now that she had taken notes at the lecture about where to find the stone carvings. Still, there were sure to be others in the neighborhood if she only looked for them. She would start with the big synagogue on 121st Street. It had a tall stone arch on the front of it, two stories high, she remembered, and along the top and sides of that arch were carved dozens of figures. Some were just objects such as a holy book and a menorah, but quite a few were animals. She thought she remembered a bull, a ram, and a thing like a fish with horns, as well as others.

Armed with pad and hard drawing pencils, she set off uptown right after breakfast. It turned out to be a very ordinary New York summer day, which meant that although the sky didn't look like rain, it also didn't look much like sky. In every direction except straight up there was nothing but pale, warm haze that was bluish toward the top of the sky and grayish toward the bottom. Probably, Janie realized, she would never even have seen the bluish part if she hadn't been looking up at the tops of buildings. In this part of the city, there were quite a few like her own building, not more than six stories, and there were some, especially along Broadway, that were only four. That made it easy to tell whether there were any carvings on them. It was much harder with the tall apartment houses, and really impossible if she were on the same side of the street they were. She would have had to be lying on her back in the middle of the traffic to see all the way to their roofs. She stubbed her toe on a crack in the sidewalk, almost stepped in a melted ice cream cone, and developed a slight crick in her neck, but she kept on looking.

She was almost at the synagogue when she made her first discovery. Halfway down the block was a brownstone house with a flight of steps running up to the second floor, and on top of each of the newel posts was a carved stone owl. The stone was rather soft and worn looking, and one of the birds had had part of his beak knocked off, but they were nice owls anyway, with big round eyes, folded wings, and strong, horny feet. Janie sat down on a parked car and began to draw the first owl, trying to make it look like a stone carving rather than a live owl. That was hard, because she could see that in some ways it was much easier to draw an owl that it had been to carve one. For example, her pencil could easily have put in a lot of small, fine feathers all over the body, such as real birds had. But the carved owl only had the feathers shown by a series of designs like downpointing arrowheads and each one of them was much too big to have been a real feather. Janie worked away, completely absorbed. Blessedly, no one came along to hang over her shoulder and ask, "What's that? Is it that stone owl? Why are you drawing that?" or (the silliest question of all) "C'n I look?" when they were already looking. The owl was really simple to draw if you stopped thinking of it as alive. She finished it and climbed up on the bottom step of the stairway to pat the owls goodbye. Then she was off to the synagogue at the other end of the block.

There were the carvings, more or less as she had remembered them, but she had something of a disappointment. Many of the figures, especially the ones at the top, were so black with grime that she could hardly make them out. She could only sketch the horned fish and the ram, which were quite near the bottom. The fish monster was wonderful. It had five horns, including one in the middle of its nose, and a tiny ship was stranded on its back. The ram was nice too, because it was standing on its hind legs to nibble the top leaves of a bush.

She looked around for something else to add to her collection and saw a dark old apartment a block away across Claremont Avenue. It was too far away to tell clearly, but it seemed to have some very heavy carving over the door and windows.

That was the beginning of Janie's wanderings. It was a great game to guess which streets or buildings would produce sculptures for her to draw. Some of the ones that looked fine from a distance turned out to have nothing but designs or leaves on them, although once she found a perfectly sweet little bird sitting on a nest in the middle of a swag of fruit and flowers. On the other hand, there were some carvings that were lumpy, stiff, or awkward and, strangely enough, they were harder to draw than the others. Usually, she didn't bother with them, because the good carvings were all around, sometimes in the most surprising places.

One surprising place was an old, run-down secondhand store on Broadway. It must once have been a drugstore, because it had CHEMIST carved very deep over the door. Above the sign was a rather large, square stone plaque with a figure that looked to Janie like the astrological figure called Sagittarius. It was a horse with a man's body, head, and arms, carrying a drawn bow. The stone was a little worn, but every line and curve was so strong and clear that Janie was amazed and delighted. It took her a long time to draw that figure because she wanted to do an extra fine job and she had never drawn such a creature before.

"Hey there, kid. What you doin' hangin' around here? You jus' tell me that, now."

Janie jumped so hard her pencil made a strand of mane run right off the paper. The voice belonged to an old man with gray bristles on his chin. He was standing so close to her he was almost on her toes and his voice sounded like the grinder on a garbage truck.

"I was drawing," she squeaked. "Just drawing. See?"

She held out her pad and pressed her back against the lamp post behind her.

"Lissen," said the man, "I own this store, see? Thirty-fi' years, an' I don' like kids, unnerstan'? Black, white, P.R., I don' care, they're all the same. Steal, break in, sell dope, get me in trouble. Now you gimme that here, lemme see it." He reached out for her pad so suddenly that she had no time to dodge. With his big right thumb, he flipped through the pages leaving a smudge mark on each one. "Animals! Lotta animals, fer chrissakes. Okay, girlie, you take yer papers an' get outta here. An' don' come back 'less you got *business*, hear me?"

For a minute she thought he was going to keep her drawing pad, but he thrust it at her flat as if he were shutting a drawer. She grabbed it and began to run back down Broadway, but not so fast that she couldn't hear him when he shouted after her. "Mind, now, I din' say those drawrin's was *bad*. They ain't so *bad*. Not bad fer a *kid*. . . ."

Janie whisked around the corner of 118th Street and sat down suddenly on an areaway step. It wasn't the running that had put her so out of breath. She was scared and mad but down inside she knew something was funny too. The man had tried to be so tough and mean but at the end it had been almost as if he were apologizing for chasing her away. Maybe it wasn't much of an apology, but he seemed to mean what he said—even if it was two different things at once.

Janie decided she might as well go home. She knew the neighborhood too well to think there were any interesting carvings between here and 116th Street. Besides, it was getting really hot out and she was hungry.

It was only a short walk to 658, now that she wasn't stopping to stare at roofs and cornices and doorways. She put down her sketch pad on the kitchen counter and rooted around in the bright, cold icebox until she found what she wanted. Then she sat on the counter eating leftover potato salad out of the container and looking over her drawings. There were about a dozen of them. One was of a doll that some child had left sitting on a windowsill, but all the rest were stone animals. She decided that the Sagittarius was the best one, even though there was something not quite right about the neck. She liked the doll too—the floppy way it sat was just right and it looked lonesome and left over.

It was very still and warm in the apartment. Janie was just beginning to consider taking a nap before dinner when she heard the sound of drawers being opened and the rattle of pencils. Mom must be home early, working in the little cubbyhole off the bedroom that had been converted from a dressing room into the offices and studio of Mary Morlan Harris, Inc. Janie slid off the counter and went toward the workroom with her drawing pad under her arm.

Mom was sitting not at the slanty-topped drawing table but at the old kneehole desk crowded up beside it. That was where she kept all her business records and the big bound book with the red leather corners where all the "money in" and "money out" had to be listed in columns. When Janie was little she had been fascinated by the idea of a book with blank pages, and one of the worst things she'd ever done—one of the things that got her in the most trouble—was to make crayon pictures all over several of the pages so that Mom had to get a whole new book and start over. That had been ages ago, though. Janie knew better now, but the idea of having a real book to draw in still intrigued her.

"Hi, Mom," she said, hooking an arm around the doorpost and swinging into the tiny room. "Are you working on the Book?" It wasn't much of a question because Janie was only about two feet away from her mother's back and could see perfectly well that the ledger was open in front of her.

"Hello, darling. I thought I heard you come in. Yes, I'm doing the Book, worse luck." She was adding up a long column of figures on her little adding machine.

"What's worse about it?" Janie wanted to know. Mom was proud of the fact that her bookkeeping was always up to date and everything balanced.

Mom sighed and stared at the figures that appeared in the window at the top of the adding machine. "Oh, nothing, hon. It's no surprise, really. But if the third quarter of this year doesn't shape up any better than the first two I'm just not going to hit the figure I was aiming for, that's all." She ran her fingers through her tawny hair so it stood out in all directions. Like a lioness, thought Janie, and knew she'd rather have red-gold hair, even standing on end, than her own obedient brown stuff.

"I brought my drawings I did today."

"Hmm? Oh yes. Were you out all this long time? Come let me see." Janie put the pad on her mother's lap.

"They're all stone sculpture things, not real," she explained quickly, as Mom looked with surprise at the owl on the first page. "A lot of the buildings around here have the wildest things carved on them." *Including this one. Especially this one.*

"Carved? Oh, I see. Of course, and you've done a good job of showing they're carved and that the doll isn't. Drawing something that's carved or painted is always hard. It's two steps away from the real thing instead of just one. These are fine, though. Look how well you've shown that the owls are free-standing but the fish-thing and the bird for instance are in relief."

Janie knew relief was what you called it when only one side was carved out of the stone and the rest was still attached. Mom had turned back to the owls. "The shading on sculpture is hard to do with a hard pencil like this. Think how much easier those stylized feathers would have been with charcoal, where you could smudge it to make shadows."

Janie considered her drawing. Yes, it was hard to do exact shadings with pencil. Although Mr. Snaith could do it, she was sure, and Mom too. She remembered an exercise Mr. Snaith had given the big kids at the art school—just drawing a ping-pong ball on a sheet of white paper. The example he had done himself was so horrifyingly perfect that Janie couldn't see how any of the students had the nerve to try to copy it. "I've got some charcoal in my big paint box," she said. "I think I have. I'll try it next time. But look at this one again. He's my favorite. I think he's Sagittarius, from astrology, you know. I didn't quite finish him. The neck part isn't right, see? On the carving it looked fine, but this keeps wanting to curve forward instead of back, and when I do it back it's too far back."

Mom had bent over the pad and was squeezing her right arm with her left hand the way she did when she was thinking very hard. She was holding a capped felt-tip pen and making small motions over the paper. Janie knew what she was doing. Sometimes your hand could tell you more than your eyes could. "It's the shoulder," said her mother. "See, darling, the line of the shoulder goes into the withers of a horse. But here the man part of him begins after the withers, not before. If you leave out the withers the poor Sagittarius looks terribly goose-necked."

Janie thought hard, trying to see the stone inside her head instead of the paper in front of her. "I get it. At least, I almost get it. But when I think of putting in the withers it just looks like the man's behind and that's wrong too. You fix it, Mom. Please show me how. I'll get you a pencil."

"Fix it? Oh, I'm not the one to do that. You should

ask Mr. Snaith. He's a real artist. You know I'm just a decorator."

Ask Mr. Snaith? For a minute Janie was outraged. Mr. Snaith wouldn't be back until the MacRae School reopened in September! Mom knew that. And inside Janie something was aching to get that drawing fixed now. She had made so many false lines she couldn't see the good one. But Mom could do it—just that one right line that would put the whole thing together. And she wouldn't. She wasn't "professional."

Instead of getting mad or begging, Janie stood looking down at her mother's hands holding the drawing pad—her neat, long, grown-up hands that never fumbled or got in each other's way. "Mom, why don't you ever draw anymore? I mean, except rooms and furniture. You used to paint all the time and now you don't even make birthday cards. *Why don't you ever do what you like to do?*" There was no answer at all as Janie turned and went out of the office.

Many of the uncomfortable little bits of the last few years came back to her now. The way she and Dad had both been puzzled and disappointed when Mom started saying she was "too busy" and "not really good enough" for painting. The way, when Dad was still teaching, he never used to come home acting tired and talking about how old he was getting. He used to read them the funny parts or the good parts of the papers he was correcting, crinkling up his eyes and waving his arms in despair or delight. He didn't do that anymore, now that he was supposed to be writing this paper, and Janie knew in the dark, fuzzy back of her mind that he was doing that because Mom wanted him to. She was the one who thought something fine would come of all this library research and the subject always seemed to come up when the Book didn't come out right.

The Book was about money. Janie wondered briefly whether the Harrises were really very poor and she'd never noticed. Certainly there were lots of people around who had more money than they did. Think of Mom's former roommate from college, for instance. Mrs. Stayman, who used to be "Aunt Elinor" before she got married and moved to London, not only wore clothes designed by a famous designer but, "She flies in for fittings, my God, my God." That was Dad talking, and Janie had the feeling that the Staymans were rich, really rich. On the other hand, there were oceans of people Janie knew who didn't have even an old stereo or a dishwasher or roller skates or roast beef *ever*. And except for not being able to go to an expensive hotel this summer instead of to Gram's for free, Janie couldn't think of anything important the family had really wanted and not been able to buy. So she didn't see how they could be poor, and that made the whole situation more puzzling.

Thinking this kind of thought made Janie's head hurt at the place where her nose joined her forehead. And now her father's voice came back to her again, saying more and more often, "I don't know what you want,

Molly; I really don't know what you want." And always the answer was: "You know, but you just don't want to face the issue." The little bits of remembering came faster, a blizzard of torn-up snapshots. Mom: "Aren't you home awfully early?" Dad: "I had about all I could take with those statistics." Mom: "Where have you *been* for two hours?" Dad: "I don't feel as if I missed much." Janie: "But Dad said he'd meet me afterward." Mom: "I'm tired of your excuses." Dad: "This summer hasn't worked out as planned—for any of us." Mom: "*Somebody* around here has to be organized." Dad: "Molly, I just don't know what you want." Mom: "Sometimes I don't know what I'm going to do with that child." Janie: "I don't know why you don't ever do what you want to anymore." Everybody: "I don't know, I don't know, I don't know." In the middle of her head one voice cut clearly through the others. "Stone is patient," said Griff lovingly. "I will be here for you always. I will be here when you want me."

II

As the weeks went by, things settled into a kind of routine, like plaster of Paris in a mold. Dad left for the library every morning as soon as it was open and didn't come back until almost time for dinner. Mom stayed home a lot to work on a long job she'd intended to put off till the end of the summer, an "industrial interior" that was supposed to make a light and airy reception room out of a perfectly square and windowless space in a skyscraper. Janie knew her mother didn't think that kind of job was very interesting, but she buried herself in layouts and almost never came out of the office to ask Janie what she was doing or where she was going. There were no fights but then nobody seemed to talk much at all except to discuss whether or not to have cold cuts for dinner or where the Sunday *Times Book Review* had gone to.

Janie had used to hate it when she found herself "just a piece of furniture" with an argument going on over her head as if she weren't there. Now she almost wished those times would come back. (Except that she didn't care, of course.) Now there were three pieces of furniture in the family. Very polite furniture they were, too, like Gram's upright Victorian chair with the rose-colored upholstery and the oval back that always resembled a pursed-up mouth.

Nobody could be furniture all the time, it seemed. They all turned back into people one weekend when they went to visit the Staymans in their new country house north of the city. Janie had never visited them before because they had been living in England and Washington, D.C., for several years. It was a pretty nice weekend, she supposed. The house had been an old mill and the Staymans were fixing it up themselves. Everything was littered with paint cans, wallpaper samples, seed packets, lengths of pipe, fluffy pink wall insulation, detached doorknobs, old bricks, bent nails, and stiffening paint brushes. All kinds of crazy things happened because nothing worked the way it was supposed to and the grownups all laughed a lot.

Nevertheless, Janie was glad when they were on the train going home. She remembered the reason why she really hadn't wanted to leave New York that weekend, the idea she'd had the week before. It was so exciting she wasn't even sure she wanted to try it out. First, she had to talk it over with Griff in the safety of the roof.

Griff was hers, and in his world things could be relied on. In his world she was always herself without turning suddenly into Janie the Bad Child or Janie the Piece of Furniture. There, air and stone and sky and steel stretched out over the earth in patterns she could begin to understand, and if she was still afraid to fly, that too could be counted on and even conquered. Because of Griff, because of Griff.

In the beginning, Janie had just assumed that Griff was special, the only one of his kind. Now, however, she knew about "the others," the carved stone animals that, like him, were "quick." Now, there was this beginning of an idea in her mind . . . the first whiff of it, like something baking in an oven. It wasn't time to take it out yet, but soon. . . .

Soon the train had arrived, soon they were home again, soon the shut-up air of the apartment enclosed them in the same polite, bland bubble they had been in before they went away. (Remember not to care.) And only a little less soon than that, about nine o'clock the next morning, Janie was up on the roof.

Since it was daytime Griff couldn't move around very much, so Janie settled herself on his back in what had become their favorite position for conversation. Between the tall wings she was nearly invisible to anyone except the pilot of a low-flying plane or a rooftop observer with binoculars. "I've been thinking," she stated as soon as she was comfortable.

"Three cheers for you," responded the griffin smartly.

Sometimes Janie wished he wouldn't talk like Evalee, but then she remembered he hadn't had many human beings from whom to learn about conversation.

"Don't be dumb. I mean really thinking. Tell me some more about how you get to be quick and what it feels like, and what the difference is between you and the ones who aren't."

"You don't want much, do you? All I can tell you, I'm afraid, is that it has to do with the one who makes us. We are made by human beings and what is in us is only what they put there. 'Quickness is a gift,' you know. From the day of carving it is either there or it is not. Maybe it goes back even beyond that to the stone itself, for everything in this world starts there. Maybe the sculptor only sees what is already formed. But without that something in the beginning there is no quickness, though it is also true that once we are quick we get more so as we get older. Some even say that the Most Ancient, as we call them, can walk by themselves without human beings to wake them, but I cannot imagine what that would be like, since I am so young myself."

Janie thought of the photographs she had seen—the Great Sphinx of Egypt smiling blindly at the sun, the winged bull with the bearded face that paced the Assyrian gateway, the white horse carved from a whole green hillside in England. She shivered a little. Yes, they might get up and prowl the world as they wished, but it was not of creatures so distant and so powerful that she was thinking now. "I don't mean just those very old ones, Griff, I mean you and the other ones you keep mentioning." She was excited now. "Is it really people who help you? It doesn't just happen?"

"Yes, I suppose so."

"Then listen, Griff, just listen. I know I'm right. I've got to be right. If you can wake up for me, why not some of the others too? There are stone animals all over, I've found them, and some of them are quick, I'm sure they are. If I tried really hard I might be able to wake them too. Then it wouldn't be just you and me."

Griff had caught her mood. He forgot himself so far as to turn his head all the way to look at her and his tail lashed once like a ringmaster's whip. "A Gathering. You are saying there would be a Gathering. The first in many years."

"Is that what you call it when you're all awake at the same time?"

"That's right. But I was hardly out of the stone when the last one happened." The griffin arched his back with pleasure so that Janie slid suddenly down on his neck. "Ah, that was a magnificent night, though nothing like the great festivals of the Old World, I suppose. Some of the Most Ancient told us about those—All Hallow's E'en in Paris, Walpurgisnacht in Vienna, and the Saturnalia." He broke off suddenly. "Excuse me, but do you think you could stop jiggling around up there? Flying with a broken primary is like carrying water in a sieve."

Flying. Janie had thought about it often, but up to now she had always drawn back from actually doing it.

She loved the feeling of space and freedom that heights gave her, yet if she went too close to an edge, if she looked straight down, if she moved too suddenly, she would be thrown once again into the whirling, spaceless fear she had felt the first time she tried to climb the pedestal at night. Griff had been very artful in getting her to follow him into high places when they played together, teasing her until her feet carried her along without the advice of her head. To him, the air was only a thinner kind of stone, so that Janie's desire to keep her feet on the ground was largely incomprehensible. Sometimes he had almost frightened her because this feeling about heights was really the only way in which they were different. Under his challenge she had forced herself further and further out. Once she had even stepped off her climbing board, where it was still braced over the gap between the buildings, and edged herself a few steps toward the front of the building, standing only on the parapet. Her face had been pressed close against the gritty side of the pedestal while her heels hung out over nothing. She still felt sick when she remembered the way the black slot behind her had seemed to draw her down and how, when she had flung herself shivering to safety, the silhouette of the griffin had loomed above her, huge and hooked.

She was still afraid, she knew, but she had worked hard since then, forcing herself to forget what might happen if she fell—or perhaps not to care. Now she apologized to Griff's primary feathers and slid carefully off his back, although the excitement was still bouncing inside her like a tennis ball. She certainly didn't want anything to happen to Griff's flying ability. Deliberately, she walked toward the edge of the pedestal, trying to look at nothing but the air in front of her face. She slid her hand along his neck but managed not to grab at him when she felt the now familiar sensation of advancing against an invisible force that was pushing her back. Instead, she stopped with her toes a good six inches from the edge. The air and sounds from the street rushed up at her and took her breath. But it *was* easier than it had been. "And it will go on getting better," she promised herself. There was nothing to hold her back anymore.

She turned and headed for the rope to the roof. "I have to go now, but I'll keep thinking about waking the other quick ones. And I'll come back tonight, Griff. I think it's time we did some flying."

12

Janie kept her promise and climbed the echoing stair-way to the roof again that night. She was ready, she told herself. She wanted to be ready. She wouldn't wait any longer.

Just for a second, when she reached the top of the pedestal, she looked down at the broad top of a bus as it crawled along the street. Her stomach gave a small twitch but she didn't let herself stop to dither. Griff was ready and she settled herself between his wings. "Put your legs forward on my shoulders," he instructed, "otherwise you'll get in the way of my wings. And hang onto my neck feathers. I won't bank or dive until you're ready. Just remember, griffins were made for the air. Here we go."

Once or twice before she had seen Griff fly, just a

few swoops when they were playing together. But this was the real thing. Her stomach had time for only one nervous twitch and then, with one great leap, the griffin took flight, catching the air with his wings just at the point where gravity would ordinarily start to pull him back to earth. They were several yards in the air before the enormous wings made their first beat. Tapered, strong, splayed, and flexible, those wings stretched out more than six feet on either side of them. They were oars and sails in one. With each wingbeat came a rushing sound that wiped away the noise of the city. They were twenty or thirty feet above the roof when Griff leveled off and swung in a circle around the water tower. Janie felt a huge joy inside her and tightened her knees on his shoulders. In the reflected light from the street and sky she saw that when Griff flew he carried his front paws half folded against his chest, the back legs flexed and trailing behind. It took only the tiniest motion of a wing to send him banking and turning, spiraling up or down. The control was perfect, graceful, effortless.

They flew slowly over 116th Street, still mounting higher in gentle turns. Leaning forward on Griff's neck, she was warm with feathers and fur, although the wind had been cool down on the roof. "Take me for a ride," she called through the wind. "Show me something wonderful."

Griff gave no answer except to quicken the beat of his wings. He seemed as absorbed in the feeling of flight as she was. Still below the tops of the tallest buildings, they slid east with the dark pillars on either side. The occasional lighted windows were single scenes sliced from different movies: colorless kitchen with an old man drinking milk, penthouse with bleeping strobe lights and people dancing, brightly lit living room with no one in it, woman with long brown hair reading alone in a double bed.

They flew to where the buildings were lower, glided out into the open, and turned back toward the Hudson. Below them the city had formed itself into a pattern of oblongs outlined with lights. They were high enough now to see the big dark patch of Central Park stretching off to the left like a slit in the city. Another, smaller patch was Morningside Park. Once, Janie had found that the darkness made heights more fearsome because she couldn't see the edges of things. But from this height the darkness was her friend. It transformed streets, avenues, roofs, and railroad tracks into an abstract design of lights and shadows.

The zigzag net of white and amber lights rippled away beneath them with a motion of its own. Except for the rush of air on her skin she felt like part of a mobile suspended on wire. Then she saw the stripes of light that were Riverside Drive and the West Side Highway, and after that the spangled surface of the river. There were not many stars but the lights of the George Washington Bridge were joined on the water by those of the high Jersey shore and the low Manhattan one. Between the bridge and a late-night patrol boat down near the harbor mouth lay a long stretch of empty river. Griff slanted down toward it, taking care not to silhouette himself against the lights in case anyone on shore were watching. The river smelled wet, warm, weedy. They skimmed close enough to see that little ripples were actually waves. Janie held her breath for one stiff moment as she thought they were going to go plowing into that gleaming darkness.

Griff didn't even get his claws wet. With a flick of a wing he leveled off a foot or two above the water and glided northward almost silently. Janie saw that they were going to go under the bridge. She held her breath again, looking upward this time. The bridge, which had seemed as slender as a string sculpture, loomed now as a mass of girders, lattice, concrete, and cables as big around as she was. They plunged under it and were swallowed suddenly by the huge roar of traffic over-head. Janie almost lost her grip on the griffin's neck in her impulse to put her hands over her ears. In that in-stant she felt that they were dropping straight toward the river through a complete emptiness. Then the noise stopped and she could feel Griff's steady wingbeats carrying them out over open water. They shot up in a steep climb, rising and rising until the towers of the bridge were beneath them. Like an even greater griffin, a bird of light, it spanned the river from bank to bank with spun steel wings.

That was the end. They turned for home, climbing in

the shadow of the Palisades and slipping over the roof-tops to 658. They landed so softly on Griff's catlike feet that Janie could hardly tell when flying turned to standing. As she went down the stairs and slipped back into the apartment she was seeing behind her eyes a pattern of light and darkness that flowed beneath her like a printed black silk scarf.

13

Janie began her quest for the other Stonefolk the next day. It was both easier and harder than she had anticipated. In spite of her confident words to Griff, she knew perfectly well that Mom would have a cat-fit if she knew her daughter was planning to roam around the city looking for stone animals. At the same time, however, she knew her mother approved of sketching just as long as Janie didn't let her see any drawings of famous statues miles away. "Ask first and miss out," as Evalee would say.

Getting away turned out to be the easy part, however. As long as Janie wasn't "moping" neither of her parents asked exactly what she was doing. All that happened was that Mom praised her for "making a real effort to get things together this summer." And that was rather a good joke.

Whenever she was at home, which wasn't too often, Janie was likely to be staring at an enormous map of the city that had come folded up in a book of her father's. The map was a great discovery because it showed not only all the streets and places of interest but also the routes of all the bus lines. Without it, she soon realized, she could never have managed her project at all. In fact, it was fairly easy to get where she wanted to go as long as she remembered to check the number of the bus she was boarding. The real problem was money. She counted her savings and found she had seven dollars and sixty-four cents, which meant twenty-one bus fares. That wasn't very many when you remembered that it took two fares for a round trip. A trip both up- or downtown and across town could end up costing as much as a dollar forty.

But the *really* hard part was picking the places to go. On her first day of hunting, she decided to try somewhere adventurous, a place where she was pretty sure to find the right kinds of animals. She wanted it to be somewhere so far away that there couldn't be any doubt about having to take the bus—otherwise she might just keep poking around the neighborhood and never get up the nerve to go farther. Armed with her sketch pad and a sandwich, she boarded a number four bus and rode to 42nd Street. There they were, the two great lions in front of the Public Library.

Janie had known the lions all her life, she guessed. You couldn't live in New York without knowing them. They were so calm and majestic with their chins sunk in their manes and their wide, mild eyes. She had always thought they must have read all the books in the library. Now, perhaps, they were considering all the world's wisdom and wondering whether human beings really knew as much as they thought they did. Surely, if any stone creatures besides Griff were more than just stone, it would be these. Yet even as she started to sketch, hoping to waken the quickness in the lions, Janie was dismayed. The lions looked so very solid and familiar in the bright July sun that she doubted whether her plan could ever work. It was a silly idea, wasn't it? A kid playing games with a stone griffin was one thing, but playing the same sort of game with public monuments was probably just going too far. Nervously, she sidled around to the other side of the north lion so the sun wouldn't get in her eyes. Well, the lions were wonderful anyway, even if they were just statues. Their manes curved around to the front as snugly as the collars of very expensive coats, and you could see the way the hide stretched over their big lion bones.

As she drew, a familiar thing happened. She forgot everything except what she was looking at—forgot the flagged terrace and the gray stone library, forgot the Krishna people playing and dancing on the corner, forgot shoppers and sightseers, strollers and students, forgot herself and the hand that drew and the pencil in the hand. She saw only the stone lions—their stoneness and their lionness and the way the two went together. Then she was sure, although the lions gave her no sign.

It had worked. Satisfied, she put away her pencil and headed uptown for the zoo.

She was nearly late getting home that first day, though she had promised herself to be very careful about the time. However, she had forgotten that walking from the library to the zoo meant going past Rockefeller Center. She simply had to stop and look at the frieze of four heraldic stone animals representing the British Isles. Then she sat down to rest on the rim of one of the fountains in the Plaza. At the top of each rectangular pool was a bronze statue of a fish carrying a Triton or Nereid on its back. They were graceful, joyous figures, and Janie stretched out her hand to the nearest one. Then she made an important discovery. The bronze was as quick as stone, though it felt different. It was warmer, sleeker, and less "patient," as Griff might have put it.

Out on the street again, she found it was the same with the bronze giant named Atlas, who carried the world on his shoulders and had the ocean wrapped modestly around one thigh.

Janie was discovering that there was a real difference between the statues, whether of stone or of metal, which were quick and those which were not. It had nothing to do with style, since some of the ones like Atlas that looked least like real figures were the easiest to find the quickness in. It didn't have to do with age either, as far as she could tell, since certainly nothing she drew on that first day was old at all, as Griff counted age.

Not until many days later, when she got to the Cloisters Museum, did she find some of the creatures that Griff might have called Most Ancient. The basilisk and the small, stiff-jointed dragon there were so old that all the sharp edges had been worn from the stone but they were so full of quickness she hardly had to draw them at all.

As the days went on, Janie's pile of drawings grew thicker and thicker. She spent most days on her project now, and even when the weather was bad she did a lot of exploring in nearby places such as Grant's Tomb and the Cathedral of St. John the Divine. The cathedral was especially good because you could sit down inside and nobody bothered you, even if you were a kid alone. Twice now when she was drawing things she had gotten the uncomfortable feeling that she was being watched. Once at the zoo, a man with a white face and eyes like prunes in juice had come right up and spoken to her. "Hey, little girl, I've got something I want to show you." Grabbing her pad like a shield, she had turned and run out of the half-deserted bird house until she could hide herself in the crowd around the sea lion pool.

That had been bad, kind of sick and scary, but nothing had come of it and she knew she was prepared now if it ever happened again. It was better, she found, if she just acted very busy and paid no attention to anyone. Even being shouted at by a nutty store owner or approached by a scary-looking man was better than being home too much. If she had needed confirmation of that she would have gotten it the afternoon she came back early because of a rainstorm and heard from the bedroom the sound of her mother crying. It sounded as if it had been going on forever without getting better, a tight, jerky noise like a broken machine. Janie hung around outside the bedroom door, wanting terribly to go in and make everything all right. At last she slid open the door but her mother was lying on the bed with her head turned away and gave no sign of knowing she was there. Janie closed the door and went upstairs to Griff, in spite of the rain.

Each day now she became surer that their plan would work. She had no way of *proving* that she had been successful in waking the Stonefolk. That would have to be done at night. But there was no question in her mind, and Griff confirmed that something in the city had begun to feel different, a kind of growing excitement. Soon it would be time.

14

One night that week Dad was almost late for dinner. They heard his key in the door just as Mom was getting ready to carve the pot roast herself. "Where's Dad?" Janie had asked unthinkingly.

It was as if Mom hadn't heard her. "Darling, get me a spoon for the juice, will you, please?"

Then Dad came in, swinging his bookbag and calling, "Sorry I'm late, gang. Just let me wash up." He disappeared into the bathroom and Janie saw her mother take a deep breath and shut her eyes for a second.

"I have an announcement to make," said Dad when he reappeared. He picked up the carving knife as if it were a sword and flourished it in a sort of salute. "Ladies and friends in the invisible multitude, you will be pleased, gratified, and properly admiring to learn that

Kenneth K. Harris (that's me, or rather that is I) has today completed the basic research for that soon-to-be epoch-making publication 'Administrative Aspects of Interim Funding in the New York City Public Schools.' "

"Yippee!" said Janie loudly. Even though she wasn't sure what all this fuss meant, it was plain that getting to the end of something you didn't enjoy doing was a good thing. "Does that mean you can have some vacation now?"

Dad finished handing the plates around. "Well, no, Jan-Jan, not exactly. I still have to *write* the, um, durned thing." He grinned at her sideways and Janie knew he was joking because he wasn't supposed to say *goddamned* in front of her. "After research comes writing," he went on, "after writing comes publication, and after publication comes, we hope, fame and fortune. Or something like that."

Janie had her mouth open to ask why writing a dull paper was going to make anybody famous or fortunate when her mother neatly blocked up the little hole in the conversation. "That's just wonderful, Ken. If the writing goes well, you might make the *Journal*'s deadline for September after all." Mom didn't sound as if it were wonderful. She sounded as if she didn't believe for a minute that the paper would be done on time.

And that, Janie observed, entirely ended the table talk for that dinnertime. The rest of the meal was like a TV show with the sound turned off. Janie was glad when she could bounce up from the table and start doing the dishes. Behind her in the dining room she heard her father say, in the tones of someone watching an interesting laboratory experiment, "You just couldn't resist that one, could you? I mean, you couldn't just say, 'How nice that you've finished the research,' now, could you?"

"Ken, what *are* you talking about? I only referred to an obvious fact. You know the *Journal* is only doing one special issue on funding. If you miss that dead-line . . ." The sentence was broken off by the sound of Mom's sandals on the floor as she left the table.

In the kitchen, Janie stood very still for a minute. The clock was still giving its tiny growl every time its second hand passed four, but otherwise there was no sound except her parents' voices. They were too faint to hear through the closed door, now that they were in the living room. Without even thinking about it, she checked the dishes stacked on the counter. Yes, there were some missing. She went to the swinging door and pushed it forward just hard enough so that she could catch it and pull it toward her as it swung back. It was really a very quiet door if you opened it that way. The near end of the dining table was out of sight from the living room and she had no reason—no reason at all—to go around to the other end.

It was a long time since she'd worried about its being wrong to eavesdrop. In her mind right now it was much more wrong for her not to know what was going on in the house. Anything at all might be happening behind her back and she would only find out about it when it was too late. She would rather be a sneaky rat than a good honest mouse that never found out about traps.

Janie stopped when she heard a new name from the living room. "What about Art?" Dad was asking. "What did he say when you called him today?"

"I didn't get him. His office says he was delayed in Brussels and won't be back for another couple of days."

"A couple of days! God, Molly, I wish we could get this thing settled. The whole situation is impossible—for all of us. I want Janie out of it, especially. And it's so unnecessary. Can't you realize that, even now?" Dad's voice was low but he was speaking with such force that Janie, sneaking dishes into the dishwasher as silently as if she were planting bombs, could hear every word. There followed a long silence in which Janie was thinking about a stone griffin. *Oh, come and take me away, please fly away with me.* But no golden, winged shape settled on the windowsill and the last words she heard that evening came through all too clearly.

"Ken, you know I've tried. I have. But I just can't see any other way. Not right now."

Janie sat in her room with the radio on as loud as she could turn it without running the risk of having some-one come in to tell her to turn it down. Of course, that didn't make much sense when she had just been going to so much trouble to listen in on her parents, but right now she had the feeling she'd heard all she could handle for a while.

Divorce. That was the word she had been thinking (and not thinking) for weeks, months now. She had heard it way back last May. It had come flying at her through the darkness on one of the nights when she'd been awakened by voices from the next room. Now, she thought, they were really going to do it. They really were. What happened to kids when their parents got divorced? She didn't know very much about it, even though she knew several people from divorced families. Some of them seemed to get along just like everybody else and some were pretty weird, but that wasn't the point. There was a big difference between *being* divorced and *getting* divorced. Being divorced might be okay if you were used to it, but Janie knew there was no way she wanted to become an expert on getting divorced. *They* might want to get divorced but she didn't. They couldn't make her. She wouldn't let them. And the first thing she wasn't going to let them do was make her cry. Sitting on her bed by the window, she lowered her head to one bent knee and bit hard on the skin at the top of it. It gave her something to think about besides the big gray patches that seemed to be growing on the summer, creeping and spreading like mildew.

She looked down at her knee and saw that she had made a large, wet purplish spot with two white half-moon shaped lines of tooth marks. The place was tender and she was going to have a black-and-blue mark. Poor knee, it isn't your fault. She put her chin on her folded arms and looked out at the parts of 116th Street and Broadway that she could see from her window. Only two blocks uptown was the former drugstore with Sagittarius on the front and a few blocks farther, almost in a straight line from her, were the two stone owls with their puffy brown feathers and round, astonished eyes. Suddenly Janie had a strong, sharp sense of all the stone animals she had been drawing over the last few weeks. All over the city they were waiting for her, on pedestals, beside steps, over doorways and windows. They were linked to her in the same way that Griff was. She could put out her hand and touch the stone of the building front which ran up to Griff, three stories above. But if Griff and the building were one, then the whole city was really just a single huge sculpture made of different kinds of stone, concrete, and steel. She was inside one piece of that sculpture now, with other parts of it stretching away in all directions to the lions, unicorns, hounds, elephants, giants, basilisks, rams, leopards, and all the other Stonefolk who were hers. The thought comforted her and she spent a long time looking out at the city's July twilight.

The flights she and Griff were making now had grown longer and swifter. She had never lost her fear of falling during a sudden steep turn, when the earth seemed to tip up over her head so that she felt like a bug about to be trapped under a saucer. However, the

joy of being free, strong, and alive at these times was so great that she kept going back to the nighttime roof as often as she could. She had come to know the city in an entirely new way, as a fish knows the ocean floor. Midtown was a high mountain to the night fliers, with lesser hills around Wall Street and the upper East Side, and one tremendous peak at the new World Trade Center.

In flight she was able to forget everything but Griff and the uncoiling mystery of the city. They almost never talked about the rest of Janie's life—"the people downstairs," Griff called them. Once, though, she had been speaking of the Stonefolk and he had been apologizing for the fact that he couldn't answer all her questions.

"At least you never tell me things that aren't so just because you think it's good for me," she said.

And Griff had turned his head to her as they flew through the starshine over Rikers Island and said, "You don't pretend or hide things from someone you care about."

That was true and Janie had no argument to offer, but the statement made her a little afraid.

15

Two days later Janie was making fruit compote after the dinner dishes were done. It was much easier than chocolate roll, and almost as much fun. Gram had taught her to do it years ago and the best part was that there was no recipe to follow. You simply took all the different kinds of leftover fruit you could find—fresh or canned—and mushed them all up together in a big bowl with their juices and anything else that seemed interesting. This time she had one soft banana, some canned peaches, some grape Kool-Aid, three maraschino cherries, the end of a bunch of red grapes, a little flat ginger ale, some sliced strawberries in white wine that Mom made for guests on Monday. Janie sliced every-thing up in the big blue bowl and was just wondering whether to put in the remains of a can of shredded cocoanut when Dad put his head in through the swinging door. "Janie, hon, would you come into the living room a minute? Your mother and I want to talk to you."

She rinsed her sticky hands and walked down the leaf-papered hall, where a griffin's face watched her from every third spray of green. In spite of everything, she knew, this had caught her unaware. She felt thin, flat, and brittle, as if there were almost nothing between her head and her legs, as if she were a paper doll that could blow away—one good puff and right out the window, out of the world. She saw Mom sitting on the sofa and almost ran to her, wanting to bury everything in her arms, wanting to be comforted again like a baby. But Mom was holding herself so stiffly that it seemed she might break in pieces if she were bounced on. So Janie sat on a chair instead because it was a formal occasion. "I don't care," Janie reminded herself. "I don't care."

Usually, when Dad said, "Your mother and I want to talk to you," it meant something serious to discuss but not a scolding—something like Why You Aren't Getting Good Marks in History or Why We Can't Go to Dixon's Island This Year. If only it would be the same sort of thing now. But it wasn't.

"Darling," said Mom, as if she were afraid to let a spot of silence start growing among them. "Darling, we . . . have an idea. We think . . . it's been such a funny summer. . . . Daddy and I thought you might like to go and visit Uncle Arthur for a while. He's been wanting you to, you know, and you always have such fun when we go there."

Janie couldn't believe what she was hearing. Did they

really think she would fall for this, that she was too dumb to know what was going on? She said very carefully, "Why would I want to go to Uncle Arthur's?"

But that was a mistake. First the game had been Let's Talk About What's Going On, Even if We Don't Say What It Is. Now it had turned into Why Is Janie Being Unreasonable? She saw something like relief in her mother's face as she started to give a list of nice, normal reasons why she, Janie, would just love to go away on a lovely visit. Janie looked at Dad and saw that his eyes were fixed on the little statue of a grazing horse she had made last year. He had on his "classroom expression," and here came his lecture, right on top of Mom's: how Uncle Arthur was having a short vacation and would take her to all sorts of interesting things that Mom and he didn't have time for right now, how she could sleep in the top bunk in the guest room and have her uncle's cat Maxim to play with, and how Mom thought she just might go up to Dixon's Island for a very short visit to Gram, who still wasn't feeling really well. It all sounded so sensible, and even, in some parts, like real fun. And there was no possible reason for her to object. Except—except that every bit of her brain was telling her not to go. "You don't know what they'll do while you're gone. Maybe you'll never see them again. It's a trick, it's a trap. There's something they aren't telling you."

To her horror, she discovered she was crying. Enormous, hot, wet tears ran out of her eyes as if out of two leaky faucets, although she was trying to keep her face as still as a statue's. It was no use, of course, and both Mom and Dad had come and put their arms around her, asking, "Darling, what is it, what's the trouble? We thought you liked Uncle Arthur. It's nothing to cry about. It's going to be fun, you'll see."

Janie was still fighting the tears, which were messing up everything. What she needed right now was to be strong and *think*—to think how to keep from being sent away and find out exactly what was going on behind this "nice vacation." Back at the beginning of the summer she had been told to cope, and she had *been* coping, she thought. But now the miserableness was spurting up inside her so hard that she couldn't say anything except, "It isn't Uncle Arthur. He's all right. It's just—" She stopped because she couldn't find words for what she knew they didn't want to hear. But already her parents were looking relieved. All along, they had only wanted her to agree, not to say what she thought.

"Well, that's fine then, darling. You see, Mother has already made plans for this trip and we wouldn't want to disappoint Gram, would we?" Janie was patted and hugged and given Dad's big handkerchief to blow on. In a minute she would be sent along to finish making the compote and the whole matter would be considered settled. Only, just as she was leaving, Dad took her by the shoulders and said, "Look, Jan-Jan, what's this all about? You don't usually blow up like this. I guess we sprang the idea on you kind of suddenly, but is something else wrong?"

She stared at her parents. There they were—two grown-up people who made it clear they weren't going to tell her the truth, didn't want the truth from her, and then asked if something were wrong. They looked as strange as trees in the familiar living room. "Oh," she said, pulling back, "it isn't anything. I mean it's just— it's just EVERYTHING."

Perhaps, she thought, as she finished with the fruit, it was all her fault anyway. She had made Mom and Dad quarrel the night of the library lecture, hadn't she? And she did forget things and leave things around too often. Maybe they would both be happier when she was gone. There was only one thing she wanted at the moment: to talk to Griff. He was always there, anyway; he didn't change.

She went into her own room and got out a good, hard jigsaw puzzle to do while she waited for her parents to go to bed. The puzzle was supposed to be a blue dragon but after a few minutes she began to suspect that some parts of another puzzle had been mixed up in it, because what in the world were all these pieces with orange stripes and spots? Somebody knocked on her door and she said, "Come in," absentmindedly. It was Mom, and she was carrying the middle-sized one of their set of red and blue suitcases.

"Darling, how about doing some packing now, while I'm here to help you? I have to go out tomorrow morning and Uncle Arthur's coming at one." She put the suitcase on the bed, opened its gaping blue jaws, and pulled out Janie's top bureau drawer.

Janie found herself on her feet so fast she couldn't tell how she got there. It was too much, just too much. "No, I *don't* want to pack. I want to do this puzzle. I want to do it *now*." She was shouting and she didn't care a bit. She felt burning hot and dangerous. She took two steps toward her mother and was not at all surprised to see her retreat toward the door as if she thought she might get burned. Mom looked shocked and Janie felt a hot little bubble of pleasure. She, Janie, wasn't supposed to be the one with the Morlan temper, but she'd show them. "Leave me alone," she said loudly, safe in the center of her circle of heat. "*Can't you even leave me alone?*"

It was nearly midnight before Janie made it up to the roof. After she'd been so mad at Mom she had rammed the suitcase under the bed and finished her puzzle. The sound of voices in the living room had told her that her rudeness was being discussed by her parents and she expected that someone would be in any minute to make her apologize. But the voices settled into silence after only a few sentences and eventually she heard her parents getting ready for bed.

Still nobody came to scold her and that made Janie feel completely unstrung. Often enough before somebody in the family had gotten mad or said mean things, although it was usually Mom who lost her temper while Janie just got stubborn and sulked. But never, never, was anyone supposed to go to bed mad. Dad said it gave you ulcers and Mom said it was bad psychology. Even when there were really big arguments, everyone always got together and agreed to "talk it over sensibly in the morning." But now—this time what she had done must be so very bad that there was nothing that could be said about it. The fear of that came down on her so hard that it squeezed out her earlier anger. Maybe she could go and say she was sorry. But now it was really late and there was no light under the bedroom door. And tomorrow they were going to send her away. It couldn't be, could it, that anything she had done was *that* bad?

"They're going to make me go and stay with Uncle Arthur," she told Griff, seating herself between his front paws. It was one of those unexpectedly cool July nights when the wind from the river smelled fresh and weedy and she was glad to hunch back into fur and feathers. It was too cool to fly, really, and besides, she wanted to talk this time. One of the first things she had thought of when she heard about going away was, "What about Griff?" Uncle Arthur lived on East 64th Street, way over near the other river, the East River. "If I go to Uncle Arthur's, will you still be quick for me? I mean, I'm going to be far away."

The griffin caressed her ear with his beak. Janie knew he really wanted to be romping around the roof or flying, but he was always very good about sitting still when she wanted to talk. "Think, little one," said the griffin. "When you first woke me you had to work quite hard and it took a long time, perhaps because you didn't know what you could do. Then as time went on you found that you didn't have to touch me for the change to happen. And if what you tell me about the other Stonefolk is right—the ones you've been hunting for in the daytime—then it is possible to start the change without ever touching us. Now you must think about something—a great secret that you already know but have forgotten. Tell me, where do we come from, all the quick ones?"

"Well, you come from the people who carved you, I suppose."

"Ah, but so does a fire hydrant or a lamp post come from a workshop somewhere. No, little one. Regardless of who made us, it was your mind that woke me and your mind that will wake the others. You know that. You know that we are yours, but you have not thought exactly what that means."

The griffin was silent for a while and Janie felt that his words had made him a little sad. It would be a strange thing to live in someone else's head. She knew that she, Janie Harris, lived in her own head, no matter what. She put an arm around Griff's neck and gently scratched the feathers under his left ear. "Griff, dear Griff. Do you think I care whether or not you are really real? You're still better. I mean, better than the things I don't make up."

Griff heaved a small sigh, and the movement of feathers under her hand *felt* as real as wet woolen mittens or freshly fired clay. Then Janie heard against her left ear a sound that might never have been heard before.

She heard the purr of a griffin, a singsong thrum from the broad lion's chest joined with a gentle, contented coo from the falcon's throat. "Well, then," he said, "there is only one more thing to say. It must be that it won't matter at all whether you are here or not. I'll be able to change and come to you anyway. At least, that's what I think. Come on, now," he added, leaping to his feet with a fanning of wings, "it's time to play."

That night they came upon a helicopter buzzing its way toward Newark Airport, and Janie found out what Griff had meant by "helicopter tag." The whirling rotors above the cabin created a downdraft of air that the griffin could ride with his wings as if he were going over Niagara Falls in a barrel. The trick, of course, was to slide out of the rushing, roaring wind at the last moment, slipping suddenly sideways before the blades came too close. Janie saw why the big machines were sometimes called choppers, but she was not afraid.

In the world of the air and the night sky she felt as if she had left behind the part of her that could be hurt, and she shouted aloud as Griff swooped downward again and again.

16

The next morning Janie woke up with a vague feeling that she would rather not. She had slept a deep, dark sleep without dreams and could have slept longer but something got into her head with the message that it was late and that there was a reason why she ought not to be found still sleeping. That was it: found when Mom came in to see about that suitcase. Uh-oh. As if being sent off to Uncle Arthur weren't bad enough. She had yelled at Mom and hadn't even been scolded for it. What could she possibly say to Mom? There was no way out of it, she decided. Much as she hated the idea she was going to have to get that suitcase packed before Mom came and did it for her. Mom would be pleased. *Wouldn't she?* And if she, Janie, were careful to put in all the virtuous things like toothbrushes and clean pajamas, there would probably be no questions asked about the rest of her packing.

The suitcase was a roomy one, so she had plenty of space for what she wanted. She was careful to put on top the things Mom was sure to check on. As a last thought, she went to her desk and got out her third best jack ball as a present for Maxim the cat. She wondered briefly whether she ought to take a present for Uncle Arthur too. But there was absolutely nothing she could think of that her Uncle Arthur would like. He certainly didn't need a shell or a book or a piece of dried seaweed. The suitcase was full and Janie was sitting on the bed beside it when she heard her mother come in the front door.

Janie wished she were made of clay so she could just be packed up in the suitcase and taken away without any fuss. She was beginning to feel it would be nice to have it over with. She wanted to stay, but she also wanted to get out. To get the hell out, she added silently. If Dad could say it, why couldn't she? Watch it. In another minute she'd be mad again, and that was what had gotten her into trouble last night.

"Janie," called Mom from the kitchen. "Are you there?"

"Uh-huh! I'm in here." Janie was puzzled. Mom sounded the way she always did—cheerful, calm, and just brisk enough so you could tell she wasn't loafing around.

"I'm coming in a minute to see about that packing," this cheerful, normal person called back.

"You don't have to," said Janie from the front hall, "I've done it already."

Mom asked her all the did-you-remember questions while the groceries were being put away in the kitchen. Janie followed her around answering and was glad to be able to say yes to everything except bedroom slippers, which were quickly found and stuffed in. "What a good girl you've been to do all that while I was out."

Then suddenly Uncle Arthur was there, fifteen minutes early. "No matter what they say, New York traffic isn't as bad as Rome's," he explained. "I always allow too much time."

Janie hadn't seen Uncle Arthur since Christmas, and she had forgotten the way he seemed to fill up whatever room he was in. As soon as he came in people stopped looking at each other and began looking at him. Not that Uncle Arthur was remarkable looking, even though he was pretty big. He wasn't nearly fat enough for a Santa Claus, not to mention the fact that he was half bald and wore glasses. But wherever Uncle Arthur was, you somehow got the feeling that he was arranging everything and nothing important would dare go wrong. Uncle Arthur's taxicabs might be early, Janie suspected, but they would never, never be late.

Uncle Arthur's way of making things go smoothly seemed to send Janie sliding out the door as if on a moving sidewalk. She was kissed by Mom and also by Dad, who suddenly turned up on his lunch break from the library, and told to remember the usual list of dull things like baths. "Now have a really super time, darling, and don't give Uncle Arthur any trouble," said Mom as they waited for the elevator.

"Trouble?" said Uncle Arthur, as if he'd never heard the word. "Now why would she do that?" And as they inched down to the ground floor and rode toward East 64th Street in a taxi, Janie decided that a person would have to be a complete dingbat to think of giving Arthur Harris any trouble.

17

Her uncle was the only person Janie knew who lived in a house in the city rather than an apartment. His house was one of a long row, all alike except for the color of their doors. Uncle Arthur owned his whole house, but he rented out the ground floor and the garden to two men who were dancers with the Manhattan Ballet Company. On the second floor were Uncle Arthur's living room–dining room and kitchen, on the third floor were his bedroom and study, and on the top floor, which used to be an attic, was the Whosis Room, where Janie was to sleep. The Whosis Room contained a double-decker bed that was reached by a rope ladder and some more ordinary bedroom furniture such as a bureau and chair, but most of it was filled with whosises, the amazing assortment of things that had come back with Uncle Arthur from the trips he took for his importing firm. Nobody, including Uncle Arthur, was ever sure what would turn up in that room and Janie remembered many exciting hours of exploring crates, boxes, and baskets.

As she began her unpacking, Janie looked around the Whosis Room and saw that there were several new-looking crates and a big something that looked like a statue, all muffled in tissue paper like crinkly snow. Janie knew that the things in the Whosis Room were always changing—being bought, sold, or given away. Before she started poking around, however, she wanted to get completely unpacked so that the bedroom part of the room would start looking like hers. The clothes were easy, but the rest of her things took longer to arrange. Finally she was satisfied. She went downstairs, grateful that Uncle Arthur hadn't insisted on helping her unpack or telling her where to put things.

She didn't have much idea of what was supposed to go on during this visit. Mom and Dad had burbled about all the neat things she and Uncle Arthur were going to do, but she had had her mind on other things. Now she had an uneasy feeling she didn't know how an uncle would expect you to act when he was using up his vacation to give his niece a "perfectly super time." (Mom's words. Was she on her way to Dixon's Island now? Without Janie, without Dad, saying, Boy, it's nice to be rid of them?)

Uncle Arthur was in the kitchen, a room almost as remarkable as the Whosis Room. Everything in it was stainless steel except for a large table made of bare striped wood. Mom was always saying that it was a true gourmet's kitchen, which was right because Uncle Arthur was a gourmet cook. That seemed to mean he ate things nobody had ever heard of and took five times as long to fix them.

Her uncle was wearing a large snow-white apron that made him look like a giant penguin. He was taking the skin off a fat, silvery fish and he greeted her as if she had been helping him to fix dinner every night for ten years. "Oh, there you are. Slice us these mushrooms, will you?" He handed her a bowl of large, lumpy brown mushroom tops, not at all like regular mushrooms, and a huge knife with a blade like a long triangle. Not a word about being careful and not cutting herself. The knife was sharp, too.

She sliced the mushrooms, watched some vegetables while they cooked in a shallow, round-bottomed skillet, grated some pepper into some broth, followed instructions for opening a bottle of wine and putting it aside to "breathe." It was all rather odd. Well, *something* was odd about Uncle Arthur. She wondered whether nobody had ever told him she was only a kid. Not that she wanted to have that rubbed in all the time, but never before had she been treated like a grown-up woman who happened to be less than five feet tall and go to Intermediate School.

Dinner tasted good, though she couldn't possibly have said exactly what they were eating. Uncle Arthur even poured her some wine. (Okay, half a glass. So he had noticed she wasn't grown up.) They talked as if they were old friends who hadn't seen each other in months and had to exchange reports on what they had been doing since Christmas. Janie heard about a big international importers' convention in Japan and the trip Uncle Arthur had taken to Hong Kong afterward. In her turn, she told about the end of school and how Alan and Evalee had gone off to Wisconsin, about what Gram had said in her last letter and about spending the weekend with the Staymans.

As she talked, Janie considered her uncle. When she was little she had been sort of afraid of him sometimes because he was so big and so very grown-up. He never played with her or bounced her around the way her other relatives and some of her parents' friends did. On the other hand, he never said any of those dumb things about how you were growing. It seemed to Janie that Uncle Arthur had become much more fun in the last couple of years. But then, she admitted generously, the reason for that could be that she was getting older and smarter. She could understand now that some people might call him stuffy. He liked to have everything in its proper place and speak in neat, orderly sentences. And what incredible words he used in his precise way. She had tried to remember some of them that evening, but gave up after "culinary," "acerbic," "execrate," "calligraphy," and "perpend." At least he didn't mind being asked what a word meant, and he always told you right then instead of saying, "Why don't you look it up?" as if you had an unabridged dictionary hanging around your neck on a string.

He was laughing now as she told him about the Staymans' house and how everything seemed more dangerous after it was fixed. He *was* like a penguin, she decided—smooth, round, solid, and solemn-looking but really very fond of having fun.

"Ellie Zueg! Oh my Lord, Ellie Zueg!" he laughed, rocking back in his chair and holding the edge of the table with both hands. (He meant Aunt Ellie, Mrs. Stayman.) "I haven't thought about her in years. Ellie the Enthusiast. I used to know her, you know, when Ken was courting Molly—your mother. They and Ken used to come and visit me in a rather bohemian place I had in the Village. Ellie was about as feather-headed as they come. I guess she hasn't changed. Your mother must have been taken aback: she takes her remodeling seriously and doesn't like seeing things mucked up by amateurs."

Janie was enjoying herself. She felt witty and grown-up. The story seemed to get funnier as she told it. "Oh, Mom was ready to have a cat-fit in the beginning, but she decided we'd just have to be very *tactful* and hope the gas stove hadn't been connected up to the airconditioning. The only really wild thing that happened was when Dad and Mr. Stayman were getting ready to put up the dining-room door. They stopped for lunch and when they came back they didn't know that Aunt Ellie had just repainted it. See, she had this big can of paint and she was wandering around and painting anything that looked as if it needed it. So Dad and Mr. Stayman got paint all over themselves and Dad said some pretty interesting things, especially when Mom started laughing at him. It was—"

The silence went on for much too long, Janie thought, but she couldn't think of any way to fill it up. She kept seeing the hurt look on her father's face and his odd not-smiling smile as he said to Mom, "If you liked this, you'll love the Three Stooges." Janie hadn't understood that. She had only seen her mother's lips press together.

"Jane," said Uncle Arthur, "how *are* your parents? What's going on, anyway?"

She twisted her napkin in her lap. If it had been paper she would have been shredding it into little paper pills. She didn't feel adult anymore. She wished she were still too young to stay up for dinner. She looked at her uncle from under her eyebrows and felt something like suspicion. Grownups just didn't ask questions like that; it wasn't the way things were. She said very rapidly, "I don't know. They thought I needed a vacation because we were all stuck in the city. Dad is very busy writing this paper, that's all." Her voice sounded like a radio that wasn't tuned in right.

Uncle Arthur was looking at her with his head on one side. It was a quiet, considering look, as if he were deciding how much to offer for a batch of Eskimo carvings or Japanese masks. But he didn't push her. All he said was, "If you look in the refrigerator, I believe you'll find two strawberry tarts."

After dinner it was already late since Uncle Arthur didn't eat at 6:30 the way they did at home. Janie decided to go upstairs to look at some carved chess sets he had brought back from Hong Kong. "Try the third crate from the back by the window. I have some work to do but I'll come up and say goodnight later."

Janie was about to start moving crates so she could get at the chess sets when she thought she would go and find Maxim to keep her company. She had seen the big brown cat lying stretched out like a fur neck scarf on the back of the living-room sofa. He might like to see the chessmen. At least she didn't have to worry about his breaking anything. Maxim was such a dignified animal that it was about as likely for him to break something as it would be for Uncle Arthur to join a rock band.

On her way to the living room she passed the lighted door of the study. She was already at the top of the next flight of stairs before she registered the sound of the telephone dial inside the study. For as long as she could remember, she had known her own phone number, AC 2-2798. It was fun to dial because it began with four twos. Zik, zik, zik, zik, zooom, zooom, zooom, went the phone dial now. But though she stood at the top of the stairs for more than a minute, there was no sound but the click of the replaced receiver. Whatever number Uncle Arthur had called, no one was at home.

18

Janie pushed back her dish and slid back on the slippery banquette. She felt smooth and cool inside as well as outside. "Gosh," she said dreamily, "I didn't know the Italians made ice cream like that." She and Uncle Arthur were in a restaurant in the Pan Am Building called the Trattoria. Janie had just finished an amazing dish called a tartuffo. It was a solid ball of ice cream rolled in bitter chocolate shavings. Unbelievable. "What shall we do now?" she asked hopefully. This was the point where most grownups would begin to get tired and want to go home. The Museum of Primitive Art had been just great but it was only 1:30, and to her the day was just starting.

"Well, Niece, I thought we would go home and take long naps. Then we'll have a lovely health food dinner and go to hear a lecture on hydraulic engineering. Or maybe. . . ."

Janie interrupted. "You're teasing me. I know you are." He had sounded just like Dad.

"I? Tease a young lady?" Uncle Arthur's eyebrows jumped up as if they were daring each other to reach his far distant hairline. He paid the waiter and they went out through the revolving door into the hot stony street.

"Umf. I always forget not to eat pasta in the summer. How about a little exercise? It isn't far to the park."

It turned out that Uncle Arthur's idea of a little exercise was to go rowing. "But you can't go rowing on the reservoir," Janie told him. "There's a big fence around it."

"That, my dearest niece, only goes to show that you are a true New Yorker instead of a perpetual tourist like me. A tourist reads guidebooks and thus acquires arcane wisdom. Come along." And that was all he would tell her.

They got off the bus at 72nd Street and strolled among the big, dusty trees. It was pretty hot even here, and Janie reflected that people who hated heat, like Mom, would have announced that it was "too hot to do anything." Not Uncle Arthur. He just walked along in his lightweight suit, as cool as—well, as a penguin. After all, he must have spent a lot of time in places much hotter than this. She pictured him stepping coolly among the sand dunes of Arabia, followed by a gasping, staggering crowd crying, "Water, water!"

"There," said her uncle with satisfaction. "If those aren't rowboats, I'm a dromedary."

Janie could see nothing but bushes so she supposed he must be able to see over them. She ran down the path but even before its end she could hear the hollow, wooden clunk of oars in oarlocks and the sound of voices over water. It was cooler. They walked to the place where the boats could be rented, or rather, Janie ran and Uncle Arthur paced steadily, as if he were going down an aisle in church.

The boats were bigger than they had looked, though of course nothing like as big as the seagoing dories on Dixon's Island. These boats were heavy and clumsy, too. Janie waited while her uncle went to talk to the man in charge.

"Uncle Arthur, can you really row a boat?" she asked doubtfully as he came back with the boat man. At that moment her uncle looked as if he hadn't seen a boat since the toy one that floated in his bathtub a long time ago in Ohio.

But already he was stepping neatly into the rowboat and holding out his hand to her. "Niece, I perceive you are a woman of little faith. You also have a poor memory. You must know that I once spent six months with your charming grandmother on Dixon's Island when I was recovering from hepatitis. That was back around the time of the First Punic War. And no one can do that without learning to row, if not to sail."

Janie wasn't quite listening anymore. She had turned

around on her seat in the bow so that she seemed to be sliding smoothly over the green-brown water. She could see the sun shining through the water in wavy slants and occasionally a little army of minnows wriggled quickly past in strict formation. Once she saw a rather large and very ugly catfish, with whiskers waving around his mouth like an underwater TV antenna.

"Of course," said Uncle Arthur's voice behind her consideringly, "I am forced to admit that rowing hasn't gotten any easier these last few years."

"Would you like me to row, Uncle Arthur? I mean just one oar. I'm good at that." Watching the water was nice but the fish weren't nearly as interesting as the ones you could see from the dock at Gram's and water so flat and still seemed almost asleep compared to the heaving Atlantic. The ocean didn't just lie down and let people row over it—it talked back.

As she moved back to sit facing the stern beside Uncle Arthur, it suddenly seemed unbearable not to be on the island. Not to be hearing the foghorns, digging for quahogs, picking beach plums, avoiding poison ivy, swimming off the dock, but most of all not to be going down with Dad to watch the little phosphorescent creatures twinkle in the nighttime tide, while Mom and Gram sat out in the cool at the top of the steps.

The oar handle felt hot and clumsy in her hands and for some reason she and Uncle Arthur never seemed to get their oars in and out at exactly the same time. The boat began to go in a zigzag wobble. "Gram always counts for us," said Janie in a small voice. They were heading for an island where a big, rustling tree leaned out over the water to make a green cave.

"So she does; I had forgotten. She taught me the same way. *One*," began Uncle Arthur obediently. "Two. *One*, two, *one*, two, *one*, two." The boat straightened out, Uncle Arthur pulled hard on his oar, and they turned in toward the little island. But before they got there, Janie felt her uncle ship his oar and half turn to look at her. She gave one more stroke, making the boat swing around in a crazy circle. Uncle Arthur reached across her and shipped the second oar. "Jane," he said. "Look at me. You look miserable. You look like San Francisco after the earthquake. Listen, child, people don't have to go on like that. I really think you ought to tell me about it."

The boat was drifting slowly into the shade, stern first. Too startled to speak, Janie looked into her uncle's face. He didn't look like a penguin now, just like a rather worried man with a broad pinkish face. That was better. Oh, much better. When she threw herself onto his chest it took them both by surprise, but he felt as solid as one of the big bollards to which boats are moored.

Janie didn't cry much this time and the tears seemed to make her feel better. She told Uncle Arthur a lot of the hard, hurting things that had been stranded in her head for so long. She told him about words that walls weren't thick enough to block, about the dumb old

children's art class where you had to be fourteen, about the paper Dad hated writing, about the townhouse job Mom hadn't gotten, and about the way the Book wasn't behaving right. "But it isn't those things. Not really. It's just that Mom and Dad and I don't—don't seem to *like* each other anymore."

There was a silence in the rowboat under the leaning tree. Across the lake four kids were clowning around and the boat man shouted to them to cut it out.

Uncle Arthur leaned on his oar and looked out across the warm green water. "Jane, it sounds as if you've been kept in the dark about a lot of this. It sounds as if we all have." He patted her shoulder rather awkwardly. "I'll have to do some thinking. Yes indeed. Meanwhile . . ." There was another pause. "Meanwhile, perhaps we'd best be getting home. That is, unless we want old candy wrappers and raw catfish for dinner. Heave ho, then." They each took an oar and steered for the boat slip. "*One*, two, *one*, two, *one*, two."

Dinner was all kinds of fascinating Chinese foods cut up very thin and cooked in a round, shallow pan called a wok. Janie was allowed to slide things around in the wok with a pair of chopsticks to make sure they didn't get too done. The result looked a little funny but it tasted fine and the shallow bowls they ate from had beautiful goldfish painted on the outside. Janie had to cheat and use a spoon only for the last little slipperiest bits. She liked Uncle Arthur's kind of cooking even better than the kind at her favorite Chinese restaurant, except that there weren't any fortune cookies. But if there had been any fortune cookies, what should hers have said? Janie didn't know.

When the dishes were done and Maxim was delicately licking up the leftover vegetables, Janie felt ready for some quiet reading. But Uncle Arthur was hovering around the kitchen doing nothing useful. Eventually he began, "Jane, I've been doing that thinking I spoke of earlier. It seems to me there are some things you ought to know." He led the way into the living room and Janie had little choice but to follow. She and Maxim went in together and the big cat, seeing that Uncle Arthur had taken his favorite chair, curled up in the middle of the carpet like a lost fur hat. Janie sat down near him because all the chairs looked much too big for her. She had a feeling of dread inside her that she didn't understand. On the way home from the lake she had felt super. Everything was going to be all right; Uncle Arthur would fix it. In a few days the pieces of the summer would come back together as if they never had been apart.

Now, suddenly, she felt very much the way she had when Dad and Mom had called her in to tell her about this "nice vacation." Something was going on and she didn't want any part of it. She almost wished she hadn't said anything in the rowboat. It was all some grown-up affair that she wasn't supposed to mess with. Well, she was stuck with it now. She waited uncomfortably, hoping to get this over with, but her uncle only sat looking closely at the palm of one large, clean hand.

"I really don't know whether I'm doing the right thing," he said at last. "I know I'm interfering, in a way, and that's a thing one shouldn't do lightly. Ah well, here I am doing it just the same. Now. What I have to say has to do with the kind of people your parents are. You know, I've known them a long time. Ken's been a lucky man in many ways. Unlike many people he's found the one thing he wants to spend his time at in his life. I didn't know him awfully well as a small child because I was so much older, but I know one thing about my brother. He's a born teacher. Of course, he didn't always know it (he thought he wanted to be a frogman, as I recall), but it was always the same. As soon as he learned to do something he wanted to rush out and show his friends how to do it too, whether it was tying his shoe or fixing a jalopy. He couldn't stop being a teacher now if they passed a law against it. But he could stop teaching for a living, and that's where things get complicated."

Uncle Arthur paused to light a small cigar. Janie had never seen him smoke before. It occurred to her that he was almost as nervous as she was. It was very strange to sit here talking about Mom and Dad as if they were just people, not parents. At the same time it was fascinating to see them in this new way.

"Now Molly is a very different kind of person," went on her uncle. "Sometimes I think she hasn't been as lucky as Ken in finding what she wants to do. She enjoys being a decorator, and I'm sure she's good at it. But there was a time—did you know, Jane, that she won a Levin Fellowship when she was only a junior in college? It would have paid her to go and study for two years with a famous watercolorist in San Francisco and her work would have been exhibited at the end. She turned it down."

Janie was bewildered. "I never knew *that*. She must have been really good. She wasn't even in art school then, not full time, and she always says if you're going to be serious about art you can't waste time on other things." It was growing dark and the big aurelia tree outside the window filled the room with a watery green twilight. Everything appeared to float a little, even Janie herself. She had stopped worrying and felt as if she could say whatever came into her head. She had a lot of questions but she thought they would be answered in time. "Go on," she said.

He didn't go on, but asked her a question instead. "How much time does your mother spend painting these days? I mean really painting, not doing sketches for clients."

"Not very much. And she gets sort of mad when anybody asks her to draw anything or says anything nice about her old pictures. You remember my picture of Sargie and the big one of Gram digging clams that's in their bedroom? She's always saying she's not 'professional.' " Janie recalled the way she felt almost mad at

Mom when she said that. "People are supposed to *like* it when you say nice things about things they've made."

Uncle Arthur looked as if he understood something. "Look," he went on, "the next part is harder. You see, I think when people get married they sometimes have very big expectations of what their life is going to be like or of what the person they marry is going to be like in fifteen or twenty years. But often things don't work out that way. I have the feeling your mother believed your father was going to be something more than a high school teacher, even a very good one. I don't know that this is a fact, but after all she had given up this fellowship, and given it up for him. I didn't tell you that, did I? I don't mean he asked her to give it up. In fact he was very upset. He wrote me a long letter about the way people should develop their talents and not hide lights under bushels, and so on. But it was too late. She had already done it before she told him about it. She said it was because she couldn't bear to be away from him for two years—they were planning to be married by then—and that was that.

"But now, years later, this school administrator's job comes along. I gather some friend of theirs is on the school board and thinks your father would have a good chance for it if he applied. It's a very good job from some points of view. No homework papers to correct, no unspeakable high school students to contend with while they try to blow up the chemistry laboratory—and the teacher. In sum, fewer headaches, shorter hours, *and* a higher salary. The only thing is, I don't think my brother cares two hoots for any of that. And I think your mother does. Not just because she wants to be rich or important. She has more sense. But perhaps she has the idea that your father isn't getting what he deserves in life. It makes her confused and resentful when he doesn't seem to want this promotion. I don't suppose he likes wasting a summer writing a dull paper just on the off-chance he can get it published. If he did get it into that journal, you see, there are some people who would think it proved he knew something about school administration. So it would help him get a job he doesn't want. But naturally he also doesn't want to disappoint Molly or have her think he *couldn't* get that job.

"I never thought of it before, but she may feel he doesn't appreciate what she's done for him—giving up that fellowship and going into the decorating business so he could go to teacher's college.

"Then a few years later you were born, and I hope you don't think it's easy having a job, raising a child, and running a house."

"I know," said Janie. "All those hats. And I try not to be *awfully* hard to take care of. Only sometimes it seems to get harder the bigger I get. I mean, when you get bigger half the time the things you do aren't even things you know are wrong." She was thinking of the night of the sculpture lecture.

Her uncle pushed down his rimless glasses and looked at her over the top of his large nose. "Are you saying you have the idea that *you* are some sort of problem? Good grief, child, you don't begin to know what bad is. I don't mean I think you're a saint. That would make us all very nervous. But I want to assure you that nothing, absolutely nothing that is happening is your fault."

She said nothing, but he read doubt in her face and made a disgusted sound. "Oh, great heavens. This has got to stop. They think they can go playing around with each other's lives and nobody will even notice. Well, that settles it. I don't know what it will be, but I really think something will have to be done."

She had to ask, even though she half knew the answer. "You mean you can't just call them up and tell them not to fight all the time?"

"Not very well. Jane, you remind me of your mother in one of her efficient moods. Let me explain something. Being an older brother and brother-in-law has its problems too. If you have spent years showing someone how to hold a bat, washing his face for him, correcting his French grammar, and laughing at his ideas about sex, you have to be very, very careful not to boss him around in later life or you stop getting invited to Christmas dinner. Nobody likes good advice as well as the person who's giving it.

"I don't mean I can't talk to them at all. On the contrary, I think I'll have to. But I'm blessed if I know what I'll say. One thing I am sure of. Since your mother's gone to Dixon's Island, we'll all have a day or so to think things over. I tried to telephone your father yesterday evening and couldn't get him. I thought you'd like to talk to him. But maybe it's just as well he was out. It will give us time to get ourselves together.

"And now I think we've had about enough of this. Has it been any help? I mean, do things seem less confusing?"

He looked so doubtful that Janie went and put her arms around him, although Uncle Arthur wasn't much of a hugger and kisser. "I don't know. I think so, but it's all mixed up. I'm just glad we went rowing."

She was so tired that as she went upstairs and got ready for bed, thoughts went flapping through her head as crazily as bats. What an amazing person this uncle was. He didn't go making phone calls behind your back, didn't think you were too dumb to know a knife was sharp, didn't try to pretend everything was fine when it wasn't. And Mom was amazing too, in a different way. She had won that important fellowship and not only turned it down, but never mentioned it afterward. She, Janie, would have told everybody about it—wanted to, anyway. Whereas Mom went around telling people she wasn't professional, couldn't draw. It was very confusing. One thing was sure, though. Janie Harris was never going to give up doing the thing she liked best and then try to make somebody else give up *his* thing so they could *both* be unhappy. No, that wasn't quite fair. On the other side of it, she also wasn't going to let anybody push her into being something she didn't want to be, just to prove she could. But then . . . Oh, nuts.

Being grown-up was certainly much more complicated than she'd thought. Even Uncle Arthur had to worry about not being a bossy older brother, while Mom and Dad could go on being married for years and not tell each other how they really felt. It could be, then, that parents didn't always know exactly why they did what they did and have it all figured out beforehand. Lying in bed, Janie opened her eyes wide and stared at the unfamiliar light patterns on the ceiling. A car went down the street and the shadow of a tree on the sidewalk flared up on the far wall and then sank down. If parents were as much like kids as that, it could be that not coming to scold someone who had shouted at you didn't mean you had given up on that person forever.

Nothing, absolutely nothing that is happening here is your fault. The thought comforted her into sleep.

19

It was two nights later when Janie decided the time had come to send for Griff. Dad had called and said Mom was due to return to the city the next day and after that something was going to happen. After that, there were too many things that could go wrong, too many possibilities she probably hadn't even thought of. As time went on, she found she couldn't get it out of her head.

That was not because Uncle Arthur had run out of things to do. They had gone walking along the East River to look at the new construction on Roosevelt Island. They had visited a little old house from Revolutionary times right in the middle of the city. They had even gone to a fantastic rock concert in Central Park, which Janie was surprised to find her uncle enjoyed very much. "After sitars in India, mouth music in the Hebrides, biwas and kotos in Japan, and hyenas in Kenya, American electric ululations hold no terrors for me." That was the way he phrased it, but Janie forgot to ask what "ululations" were. A blank feeling had settled on her after the day they went rowing and the thing she remembered best about those two days was the life-size bronze statue of the husky dog Balto that they had passed in the park on the way to the concert. They had not had time to stop and look, but she had been able to tell at one glance that the statue was quick. In the daytime world there was nothing she could do about anything, but to Griff and the other Stonefolk she was powerful and important.

She was thinking now of all the stone and metal creatures in her sketch pad. She had been going through the pad as she sat in the living room after dinner, remembering the adventures she had had in her wanderings. She got up from her chair and her uncle looked up from the stack of importer's catalogues he was marking. "Off to bed already? I was going to ask whether I could look at your sketches later."

"Oh sure. Could I show them to you tomorrow? It's after nine thirty and that's when I usually go to bed." She tried to sound as vague as possible because she really didn't want any questions. (Although Uncle Arthur, of all people, might possibly understand about Griff. Might.)

"Oh, is it? Well, then, sleep well." He gave her the special smile that meant tucking his chin into his neck and pushing his glasses down his nose. It made him look more than ever like a penguin—one that was trying to look down over its stomach at an egg it had just laid. She didn't mind when he didn't reach up to kiss her. Some people were always hugging and grabbing and it didn't mean a thing. Besides, the fact that he wasn't a big goodnight man meant she could be sure there would be no late night visitor to discover that she wasn't in her bed.

The way to the roof was by a ladder in the back of a big closet in Janie's room. This roof was much smaller than the one at home, of course. There was just the trap-door in one corner and a brick chimney in another, with the inevitable sooty black roof surface between them. The parapet around it was only about two-and-a-half feet high. Janie put one leg over it and sat astride, with her back against the chimney. In this position she was facing west, more or less toward Griff. For a long time she sat staring at the last dribbles of sunset and thinking about the stone griffin, but it was hard, harder than she had thought, to summon the picture of him into her mind, and the sky remained empty of bronze-colored wings. She shut her eyes then and remembered with her fingers rather than with her mind. Yes, when she had scrubbed him clean that first day, and when she had sat or climbed on him so many times later—*that* was the way the ridge of feathers ran along his eye-brows, the shape of the knob at the back of his elbow, the way his ears grew thin at the tips. She had been concentrating so hard that she never heard him coming. She felt only the backwash of air as he landed and then her own relief. "It worked!"

"Of course it worked. I told you it would. It only took a little longer." The griffin was in fine form, his ears erect, his tail twitching eagerly. He leaped to the top of the chimney and flapped his wings until the leaves of the aurelia tree rustled and two indignant pigeons flew sleepily off to a safer roost. "Is it to be tonight? The Gathering? Say it's tonight," he urged.

"Yes, it's tonight; it has to be. But, Griff, I don't really have any idea how to start. It took me so long to bring you here. Do I have to sit and call each one of *them*? That would take hours."

"What? Sit around on a night like this, with the stars as big as waterlilies and the moon coming up like the king of the golden carp? We fly, my friend. So get up, hold tight, and remember, 'The world may tip and the world may slope, / But the flier is always rightside up.' "

"That's not an awfully good rhyme," Janie objected as they took off. "Is it another saying of the Stonefolk?"

"It's a griffin saying, roughly translated from the Sumerian. I learned it from a friend in the Brooklyn Museum. Where do we go first?"

It was not quite completely dark when they took off, flying west and north to the area around 116th Street where Janie had first begun her hunt for the Stonefolk. By the time they had located the first two or three of the stone carvings, she wished she had brought her sketch-

188

book with her. It was hard to remember exactly which block was the home of this or that creature and she was afraid she might miss some. The first few were difficult to waken. The two stone owls in front of the brownstone stayed wrapped in stony dreams for long minutes while Janie stood in front of them and Griff lurked in the shadows of an areaway. At last she felt the first irritable, birdlike twitches that told her she had succeeded. When she reached the old drugstore, the Sagittarius was easier. He leaped lightly down to the pavement and bowed his man's body and horse's forelegs to Janie, where she and Griff and the owls perched on the building's roof line. There were still people on the streets at that hour. Janie realized suddenly that they were bound to be seen if they kept traveling together in a group. Naturally, the Sagittarius—and the ram and horned whale from the synagogue—couldn't fly. The whale, in fact, seemed to swim through the concrete sidewalk surface. But although those three were small enough to hide in the shadows, she had an uneasy vision of what would happen when they got to the bronze dog Balto, the Library lions, or the gigantic figure of Atlas with the ocean wrapped around his thigh. "We'll have to think of a place to meet later, when we're all ready," she said. "What about—I know, that big place in the park. They call it the Sheep Meadow. We'll have the Gathering there."

She sent the owls to deliver her message to the creatures on the sidewalk. "Come back in case I need you again," she asked the owls. "You're much harder to see than Griff and I." The owls giggled and twittered together but said they would be glad to stay. They seemed to be rather silly creatures, fluffing up their feathers and rolling their big yellow eyes. Janie whispered to Griff that they might not be very reliable messengers. "Young," whispered Griff to her disapprovingly, "very young. Not more than a couple of decades old and made of soft stone, to boot. It will be a long time before *they* learn the patience of stone."

Then the four of them flew on through the warm, watery night, skimming quickly along the routes it had taken Janie so much time, planning, and bus fare to travel before. At the Cloisters, perched on its rocky crag, a huge, curved three-quarter moon the color of a goldfish swam up over Brooklyn. It seemed to Janie that the quickness in those old stones made a funnel that drew them down into the courtyard. The basilisks, lions, dragons, wyverns, hounds, deer, leopards, serpents, and others appeared almost to know of their coming in advance. They fled past the heat-sleepy watchman and down the rocks toward Central Park like shadows on the stone.

The further she went, the easier Janie found her job was. By the time they had finished with the Columbia campus, the Cathedral, and the fantastic, funny buildings on the West Side near the park, she had found she could call the sleeping forms without even being able to see them clearly, far less touch them. And she had been right about the metal statues as well. "I see you have quickened some of the Fiery Ones," commented Griff, nodding down at a small cast-iron dragon that was keeping pace with them through the air.

"Yes, but they seem a little different from you Stone-folk. Why do you call them the Fiery Ones?"

"Because they are born in fire. Metal is only a special sort of stone, of course, and we were all molten in the beginning. But they must be melted again before they are formed. It makes them strong and fierce, wild and lively, though they are not so long-enduring as we are. Metal corrodes eventually, so few of them last out the centuries and learn real patience. Nevertheless, they are cousins of ours and all right in their way."

Griff swung low over the Sheep Meadow on the way to the Metropolitan Museum of Art, and she could see that the broad, sloping space was already filling up. In the light of the outsized moon the shadowy forms seemed to slide back and forth between flesh, fur, or feathers and the still, sharp-edged lines of statues.

There was no open courtyard at the museum, and of course no hope of getting inside after hours. They came down softly on the roof beside a set of sloping skylights and, looking in through a crack, Janie saw they were over the medieval wing. That was good. She set herself to remembering the creatures she had found in her day of wandering the endless halls and corridors. Before she had been at work very long, however, she could tell that something strange was happening. It was not only the creatures she had already found who came to her call. Others she had never seen were joining the crowd that trotted, prowled, slithered, and winged toward the meadow. There were just too many for her ever to have sketched in one day; she hadn't even been able to check on every single hall and most of the Egyptian wing had been closed. Janie felt a wave of excitement rise in her as she watched them come, stretching and leaping in their new freedom. She felt her power grow, so that she could reach out and touch the secret life in all the creatures, stone or metal. She called to Griff that they must hurry on.

They flew over the rest of the park, where some of the statues were quick but some were nothing but lumps of stone and metal. At the park's southern entrance, Janie saw two great, fiery horses leap joyfully from beneath their frozen riders and gallop north toward the Sheep Meadow, neighing like bronze bugles. Then Griff was banking toward Rockefeller Center, the Church of St. Bartholomew, and the Public Library. As they swung down, she saw how much of the city she had had to leave out. There were pieces of Manhattan she had never been near, not to mention even bigger stretches of Brooklyn, the Bronx, Queens, and Staten Island. They had stopped to rest for a minute on the roof of 666 Fifth Avenue. It was windy up there. She put out a hand to Griff's neck to steady herself. The darkness made it hard to tell what was solid and what was air. The building seemed to taper down to toothpick size below her and she felt a moment of the old empty fear. Then her eyes were able to fix themselves on a large federal eagle that flapped northward from the courthouses downtown. The big bird was weighed down by a large heraldic shield clutched in his claws. Janie spared one regretful thought for the parts of the city she had missed. She climbed back onto the griffin, scolded the two silly owls for playing tag with a passing helicopter, and set out after the eagle for the park.

20

It was truly a Gathering, Janie thought as they landed on top of a small knoll in the Sheep Meadow. When she got down from Griff and began to walk around among the Stonefolk and the Fiery Ones, she discovered that her suspicion had been right. Not only were there beasts she had never seen before, but many of those who had been carved small had grown back to normal size. She saw the Sagittarius from the drugstore and called to him delightedly, but he didn't seem to recognize her words and came over only when she caught his eye. He was no longer the size of a terrier, but had gained the full stature of a horse. His bow was slung over his shoulder and he bowed to her again as he had on the sidewalk, although this time the gesture was much more impressive. "Chiron greets you, Mistress of Stones," he said in a deep voice.

Janie was delighted. She had a title, like Miss Universe or the Most Valuable Player. She tried to answer in the same important-sounding language. "The Mistress of Stones returns your greeting. But tell me, who is it that you say you are if you are not Sagittarius?"

He folded his arms and smiled at her kindly. "Sagittarius is indeed my cousin, Mistress. But I was made in the likeness of Chiron, an ancient centaur famed as a teacher of medicine. That is why you found me in a frieze above a place where medicines were once sold.

"But come now, it is wrong of me to keep you talking when the other Stonefolk are waiting to meet you. It is long since the one who called us forth was so young in the years of the world." He half turned toward the crowd that stretched away over the meadow and Janie saw there was indeed quite a press of creatures around them. With the centaur on one side and Griff on the other, she began to move across the grass. At every turn she saw old friends from the sketchbook or fascinating new faces. The iron lion with the curly mane had left his lamp on Riverside Drive and was playing tag with the dog Balto and the mountain lion from near the 66th Street playground. The stone creatures, she saw, tended to ignore the metal ones, whom they greatly outnumbered. The latter didn't seem to mind, however, and played with each other very cheerfully.

A tremendous splashing was coming from the lake at the north end of the meadow, the same lake where she and Uncle Arthur had gone rowing. The six Tritons and Nereids from the fountains at Rockefeller

Center had found the water and were spouting, shouting, and blowing on conch shells. With them was the
horned whale from the synagogue. "A leviathan," explained Chiron. "It is fortunate he hasn't grown as I
have; he'd fill the lake." One of the gold eagles from the
front of the Waldorf-Astoria Hotel came flying up with
a bronze dolphin held carefully in his claws. The dolphin
dove shimmering into the lake and rose to call his thanks
for the lift. He swam over to where Janie stood on the
edge of the mall and raised his frilly head toward her.
"Have you seen the other fish?" he asked anxiously.
"We all live together with the Tritons and Nereids but
I don't see Sturgeon and the rest."

"Silly Dolf," cried a metallic voice from the water.
"We got here way ahead of you." A porpoise swam up
to them, looking very pleased with himself. "The giant
brought us," he explained. "You know—Atlas, from
630 Fifth Avenue. All these years and he remembered
how we almost missed the last Gathering. I don't know
why giants have such a bad name." The two swam off
to join their friends.

"By the way," said Janie to Griff and the centaur,
"when was the last Gathering? I keep meaning to ask."

"Well," began Griff, "the last one *I* attended was in
1934. I was hardly out of the workshop then, of course."
He gave a respectful nod toward Chiron. "There may
have been others that I wasn't old enough to tune in
on."

"Griff, why do you always act as if Chiron knows

more about the Stonefolk than you do? I thought you all got wiser and more quick when you got older, and I don't see how Chiron can be much older than you. You say nothing is very old in New York, unless it's in a museum."

The griffin raised his wings in a gesture that was like shrugging his shoulders. "Ah well, you can't know everything, can you? Chiron is one of the oldest creatures here. Older, maybe, than any living person knows."

"It's true," confirmed the centaur. "I wasn't made for that pharmacy on Broadway. I was brought to this country by a man from Rumania. In the town we came from, the man and I, I was part of the village church, an old stone church from the Middle Ages. I was set in the wall of the church behind the pulpit, and when the soldiers came and destroyed both the church and the village, the canopy over the pulpit sheltered me from falling stones and timber. When at last the wall collapsed, I was shaken free, almost the only thing in the village left whole and unscorched. And the man, who was a boy then and had run away to the hills, came back and found me and brought me with him all those miles to this city. He kept me safe until he had saved enough money to open that pharmacy and build me into its doorway. But you see, I was old long before that. I was old when they dug me out of the ground and put me behind the pulpit of that Rumanian church. I was carved by a Roman sculptor in the days when Rumania was part of the Roman Empire. When the legions left and the temple of Aesculapius fell to ruin, the people roundabout used it for a stone quarry. The stonemasons from the monastery found me and used me for their new church in the year 1204."

The centaur's voice trailed off into silence and Janie saw that he was dreaming of times long past, standing so still that he seemed about to go back into stone. Then he shook himself like a horse bothered by flies. "A long time ago, that was. *Forsan et haec olim meminisse juvabit.*"

"Was that *Latin*?" whispered Janie, nudging the griffin.

"Don't ask me," he hissed back. "I'm only fifty-three, remember?" But the centaur was still speaking.

"Yes, I have been to more Gatherings than I can count. But there have been fewer and fewer in recent years. Not many persons even bother to look at us any-more, much less to quicken us. After the Gathering of 1934, there was only one other, and it was small. The old man was a composer of music and had great vision, but he was weak and tired and in the hospital. Only a very few of the oldest and quickest of us heard his call. That was in 1945 and he died soon after. There has been no Gathering since, though there may have been one or two single cases. Much has changed even in so short a time as the hundred years since the not-mad poet lived in Brooklyn and there was a Gathering every year."

As Chiron spoke, they were walking together around

the edge of the crowd, with various creatures coming up every minute to offer Janie a paw or hoof or claw. Unicorns gave their horns and snakes writhed themselves into elegant spirals of greeting. For some time Janie had been dimly aware of the two great lions from the library. They seemed to be trotting everywhere and asking questions of each group of creatures they met. Now they gave two triumphant roars and she saw what they had been searching for. Two graceful stone lionesses came bounding out of the crowd. There could be no doubt that this was a reunion. Each pair leaped, rolled, licked, and wrestled with blows that only a lion—and a stone lion, at that—could have survived. Janie remembered suddenly that she had seen the two lionesses from the bus one day as she rode up Madison Avenue past the Morgan Library. It had been impossible to stop right then because she was on her way home from City Hall, so she had been forced to leave them with only a glance. Yet here they were anyway, and Janie was glad as she watched the puppy-like gambolings of the usually dignified males. My goodness, she thought. I wonder whether they'll have stone lion cubs. The young ones could sit outside bookstores.

The two excitable owls who had kept them company earlier that evening flew up and stalled with their wings so that they landed on Griff's back with two thumps. "Are there enough? Are there enough?" they hooted. "Everyone is talking about forming the Circle, but are there enough?"

"Enough for what?" cut in Janie.

"Enough of *us*, Mistress," explained one of the owls. "The Circle doesn't work if there aren't enough." He tried to bow as he spoke, nearly fell over, and dug his claws into Griff's back to steady himself. There was a startled griffin squawk and Janie was blown back against Chiron's side by the wash of air as Griff flapped ten feet into the air, then settled back, shaking his wings. "When were you owls *made*, anyway? Last year?" he exclaimed, and Chiron turned away to hide a smile.

"It does look to me as if the Number has been reached," said the centaur over his shoulder, "but of course that is for one of the Most Ancient to say. I saw Horus the falcon earlier. Go and ask him."

The owls fluttered into the air (they had not been shaken loose by Griff's leap). However, it was clear that the decision had already been made without them. All over the meadow the Stonefolk and the Fiery Ones were forming a series of circles, one inside the other. They moved hesitantly at first. Then as the rings were completed they swung into motion, one circling left, the next one right. Above them the circles were repeated in the air by the eagles, harpies, falcons, swans, dragons, angels, and small birds.

Janie and her two companions headed toward the circles, as stragglers from all over the meadow were doing. She saw that Griff's keen eyes were fixed on the wheel of wings overhead. "Look," she said, "there are the two griffins from 36 East 72nd Street. I was hoping they were here. Go on, fly with them. I'll be all right with Chiron. I'll be able to see better down here."

Griff was in the air almost before she finished speaking. "I will be watching you," he called. "Don't lose yourself." With four beats of his wings he joined the wheeling fliers.

Janie and the centaur went on toward the circles. "I think Griff must be too young to have seen one of these before," she said. "Tell me about the Circle and the dance."

Chiron gazed up at the huge moon, that now seemed to hang right over their heads. "It is not a thing to be spoken," he said slowly. "It is a secret knowledge that comes to us gradually, as clay turns to limestone."

"But you can tell me," she said with certainty. "I am the Mistress of Stones."

The centaur looked at her out of wise brown eyes that had a blue sheen on them like a horse's. "I was not forgetting that. I only said the secret should not be spoken. But surely you must know it, for you are indeed the Mistress."

Janie watched the moving circles, turning faster now and changing direction in a pattern that seemed always on the edge of showing itself. "I know," she said softly, "I really know. But tell me anyway."

They were standing on a small knoll below which lay the meadow and the dancers. All around Central Park rose the tall, quiet buildings, making a last, outermost circle of standing stones.

"The Great Circle," began the centaur, "is a motion without motion. In the universe, too, all things revolve and are still. As the stars move above, so do we below.

For what are the stars but stones, and in each stone is a star. Each separate circle is only part of a greater one. That which is soft becomes stone. That which is stone becomes dust. All in the Great Circle."

He fell silent and as she watched, Janie saw that the circles had ceased to move against each other and were all moving in the same direction.

"It is a spell," she said, echoing the centaur's tone. "It is a magic for making things come together." The knowledge came to her from some hidden place in her mind. She reached up her hand to Chiron's and together they walked into the outermost circle. It opened to receive them and Janie's left hand was taken by a limestone St. George, still twined with his dragon.

Something was happening beyond the Circle. It was opening and closing, opening and closing as it had for Chiron and Janie. The figures that were now joining the dance must have come from far away, Janie reflected—too far for her to have been anywhere near them. It was the dance itself that called them together, and they were the most ancient and powerful, the quickest of all. There came bulls with discs between their horns, sphinxes, nine-headed cobras, a chimera, and a solemn figure with a man's head on a bull's body. The motion of the circles grew swifter.

Between the saint and the centaur, Janie circled, moved by a rhythm more powerful than music. The circles had become a single spiral, winding always toward the center. At that center, glimpsed between the shifting figures, stood something bright and still. Janie saw it take shape slowly, like a lamp that is approached along a corridor. When it was clearly visible the circle of creatures raised a greeting. "Sekhmet! Sekhmet! Lion Queen! Mother of Darkness! Lady out of Time! Spindle of the World! Sekhmet!" In the center of the spiral stood the lion-headed goddess of Egypt, the true Eldest One. Her lion's face blazed with white light and in the hands crossed on her breast she held the crook and flail, symbols of royalty. In wound the dancers, now a double spiral—one on the earth and one in the air. As each one reached that bright center the goddess stretched out her hand and spoke. Now Janie could hear the words. "Receive the blessing of Sekhmet. Stone upon you. Receive the blessing of Sekhmet. Stone upon you." Her voice was as sharp and beautiful as diamonds or the claw of the lioness raised against the sun.

Ahead of Janie the hand of the goddess was raised over St. George and his dragon and they faded away into darkness. "Stone upon you." Janie tried to hang back, then she was face to face with Sekhmet.

"Welcome," the heatless voice said to her. "Do you not know me? We have met before."

"Yes, I remember. I saw your picture in a book."

"You were mine, then and now. You will be one of us."

The goddess was smiling, her hands stretched out in welcome. *One of us. One of us.* "No," said Janie desperately. "I can't. I'm a person."

"But you have wished this. Many times. And you have worked bravely and secretly to bring us here. We would reward you. Remember, stone is patient. Stone is hard. Stone cannot be hurt. We care for you more than the others do. Come and be ours forever." The bright hands stretched toward her.

Janie saw that she would have to fight. The game was not hers any longer. "You can't," she cried. "I am the Mistress of Stones."

There was no change in the goddess's face. "That is nothing to me," she said, smiling still. "I am the Mistress of Mistresses. Come."

"Griff, Chiron, help me!" But the answer of the crowd was only, "Be one of us," and even Chiron was smiling down at her with eyes like her father's.

"Mom, Dad, Sargie! Gram, Uncle Arthur!" she cried silently, and got no answer. There was only one person who could help her now.

"I am myself!" she shouted, as Sekhmet's brightness advanced to engulf her. "I am not the Mistress of Stones. I am myself. I make things." She gulped for breath in air that seemed to have turned solid. "*I made you*," she called to the Stonefolk. "*I can stop making you*. I will never call you again, do you hear?"

She turned her back on them all and ran blindly out of the circle.

From behind came a terrible, slow bolt of light, which took her and tossed her high above the meadow. There was a silent cracking of the air like that which is felt just before thunder. The force of her rising lessened as the fingers of gravity reached out for her. Heavy as stone, she fell back toward earth—and was caught, cradled, and lifted by something combining fur and feathers. She sprawled across Griff's back and felt the huge muscles of his shoulders fighting to balance them both. "Meanwhile," said a voice in her ear that didn't sound quite like Griff's, "perhaps we'd best be getting home." She opened her eyes and saw that below them in the Sheep Meadow the burning pillar that was Sekhmet had vanished completely. Across the grass lay only a faint wet shine, like the phosphorescent ebbing of a summer wave.

21

It had nothing to do with dreaming, Janie realized when she woke up the next morning in the Whosis Room. She had had dreams, of course, difficult, twitchy dreams in which everything seemed to be vaguely out of shape. But the feeling she had now did not come out of the dreams. Something was finished, done with. She felt the way you did at the end of the movie when you went back out into the too-bright daylight, blinking and trying to remember what was supposed to be going on out there.

Today was the day when Mom got back from the island. It was the day when Uncle Arthur was going to talk to her parents, and there was no way she could get out of that scene—not by turning herself into stone, not by being a baby and crying, not by listening at doors so she could know and not know at the same time. There was to be no more avoiding things. It was something of a relief to have that settled. She went downstairs and was immediately confronted by another crisis.

Not that it looked like a crisis at first glance. All she saw was her uncle sitting in his oversized chair and leafing through something on his lap. It was her sketch pad, the one she'd said he could look at, the one she'd left in the living room yesterday evening. It was the sketch pad with the drawings of sculpture that certainly didn't come from the neighborhood of West 116th Street. Kids her age weren't usually allowed to wander around alone. And Janie had never thought her Uncle Arthur was a fool.

She went into the kitchen and got herself a piece of fresh date bread and a glass of milk. As an afterthought she poured her milk into a mug and added quite a lot of strong coffee from the Chemex on the stove. She thought she was going to need it.

There was nowhere to sit in the kitchen. Besides, she had meant to start this day by not avoiding things. She went in and sat at the dining table in the end of the living room. There was no sound but the turning of pages until she was almost through with her breakfast.

"You can take your shoulders out of your ears," observed her uncle mildly. "I seldom eat nieces on Fridays. I shall merely remark that (a) you draw very well and (b) you seem to have had a very peregrinatory summer."

"Pere—what?"

"Peregrinatory: moving about, migrant, not staying still. In short, you've been wandering all over the city and I'm not even going to ask whether anyone went with you or whether your parents knew about it. It was a very foolish, possibly dangerous, thing to do. But I suppose I'm curious. How did you manage it? You can't just have walked. There's an eagle here that's from the pediment of one of the courthouses down by the Brooklyn Bridge, unless I'm much mistaken."

"Well, I took the bus, some of the time. I used my allowance and some other money I had. And Dad had this big map—*a* big map—of where all the buses went. I got lost a couple of times, but it didn't matter very much because there were things to draw all over. You see, I got interested in drawing these stone carvings and then I ran out of things to draw around home so I, uh, just went," finished Janie, running out herself.

"Mmmm. And didn't it seem to you that your parents might be worried about you if they thought you were gadding about alone in the second largest city in the world?"

"Well-l." Janie was uncomfortable now. "They didn't ask me, so I didn't tell. I mean, Mom said she didn't want me to stay inside all the time and"—she ended in a burst of honesty—"it wasn't much fun being home just then anyway." She was twisting her hair again. Deliberately, she let the limp lock unwind itself and sat up straight. "I guess you'll have to tell Mom and Dad, hunh?"

Uncle Arthur got up and went to collect the mail

that had just popped in through the slot in the front door. "I don't know. I suppose I'd make a poor parent, but this is the way it seems to me. There may be things you haven't been telling them this summer, but there are also things they haven't been telling you. I'd say it was about even. 'No further questions,' as they say in court."

Janie got up, relieved, to take her dishes into the kitchen. But all the time she was putting them in the dishwasher and making herself a cucumber, lox, and cream cheese sandwich for the trip they were going to take to the Aquarium, she could see her uncle leafing again through the sketch pad. He spent the longest time on the last few pages—the ones where she had drawn Griff flying and some large views of the city at night, the way it had looked from the air.

It would probably be a long time before Janie could be comfortable thinking about fish after their day at the Aquarium. The creatures that lived in the big tanks were beautiful or weird or fascinating, but she couldn't concentrate on reading the information on the labels. Each dim green tank was like a TV screen when you turned it on in the middle of the show and couldn't follow the story.

Once they stopped in front of a tankful of piranhas, those South American fish that were supposed to be so fierce and hungry they would tear a swimmer apart in less than a minute. Janie had heard of piranhas and had imagined them as something like hundreds of tiny sharks, but they weren't. They were very pretty, flat, shiny fish like silver dollars swimming on edge. As she and Uncle Arthur came up to the piranha tank a dumpy man and his wife were just leaving. "Aw, c'mon, Margaret," said the man. " 'S nothin' to see here. They're no fun 'nless they're eatin' somebody."

All day Janie kept shivering whenever she remembered that remark. She was thinking about it again after lunch when Uncle Arthur stepped into a phone booth and telephoned her parents. Just like that. She supposed she had figured her uncle would go off to his study that evening and have a long grown-up talk with Mom and Dad sometime when she wasn't around. She should have known that wasn't his way. So here she was standing inside the open door of a phone booth on the boardwalk in Coney Island and hearing her uncle say, "Molly dear, it's Arthur. How was the trip? Restful, I hope. . . . And how is your wonderful mother? Fine. Yes, speaking of wonderful people, she's fine too. Absolutely no trouble. You deserve to be philoprogenitive. . . . Oh, that's to be loving of one's children. Well, we're halfway through my only dime and I have something on my mind. I don't know what you and Ken have worked out, if anything, but it's beginning to seem to me that the time has come for a little family council. No, I mean it. . . . Yes, of course including Jane. You have a pretty concerned party here, you know. . . . Yes, she does. . . . Well, what did you expect? And while we're at it, you have a pretty concerned brother-in-law as well. . . . I was thinking about tonight around seven.

Both of you. Is that all right? . . . Molly dear, how are things? I mean really . . . um . . . very good. All right, we'll talk about it tonight. . . . Want to say hello to my niece? Of course, she's right here. . . . Sorry, what other way would you suggest? Here she is now."

Janie had trouble later remembering what she and Mom had actually said to each other then except that Mom asked her at least three times whether she were all right and ended with, "I'll see you tonight, darling, I guess. Daddy and I have missed you *so much*, both of us. Love you. 'Bye."

After that, she guessed it wasn't surprising that both she and Uncle Arthur were rather thoughtful for the rest of the afternoon. They watched the white whales in the big pool that was built so you could see the whales under water. Then they went to the dolphin show, where trained dolphins did tricks for a girl in a bathing suit. In the middle of the show Janie said, "Uncle Arthur? Am I supposed to . . . do you think I ought to pack when we get back?"

"Pack?" said her uncle, keeping his eyes on the firm-bodied, flexible black-and-white dolphins as they leaped and arched through the water.

"Yes. My stuff, my suitcase."

"Oh, your suitcase. Jane, I just don't know. I suppose so. Why don't we wait and see?"

As they left the Aquarium, Janie found he had put an arm around her shoulders. It was quite a long walk back to the subway and neither of them thought of anything to say.

22

It was five minutes to seven when Janie, fidgeting around the front window, saw her parents walking down the block. "They're here!" she called. But before she reached the front door her feet had slowed and she said to her uncle, "What am I going to say?"

"I'd start by telling them how much you've missed them."

As it turned out, however, she didn't have to worry about that. As soon as the kissing and hugging and how-are-yous were over, before they had even sat down, Dad turned to Uncle Arthur and said, "I've got just one thing to say before we get into this. I guess we're all feeling about the same way I do. I haven't been in such a state since a certain famous high school debate in 1952." The three grownups laughed a little uneasily, and they all sat down in the living room, with Janie on the floor again. It made her feel too conspicuous to sit in a chair—like a skyscraper sticking up in the wind and weather.

There was a little silence until Janie's mother leaned forward over her clasped hands and said, "Well, I guess it's hard to know where to begin. Janie, darling, Daddy and I are both feeling a little dumb. I mean, we had no idea you knew we were—were having some disagreements."

Dad opened his mouth to say something, but closed it again like a drawer of unpaid bills.

"I know," said Mom quickly, "it was more than disagreements. And you did tell me we couldn't go on trying to keep things from her. But, Janie, we neither of us thought you had the slightest idea and we didn't want, really we didn't want, to upset you. So let's see if we can't straighten this out. Tell us what's been bothering you and we'll see what we can say about it."

So Janie told it again, the way she had to Uncle Arthur in the rowboat, only this time it was a little easier. Of course, there was a lot she couldn't say, either. How could you describe what it was like to be a piece of furniture, for instance? But she told about hearing things and about Dad's not coming home for lunch anymore, and jokes that didn't make anybody laugh, and going out to sketch and not wanting to come home. ("Oh darling," said Mom. "Oh, Janie, my own baby!") Finally Janie told about wondering why grownups made themselves do things they didn't like and gave up things they did like.

She was in her mother's arms by that time and Dad came over and held her too, saying, "My God." Then he said, "Dumb, dumb, dumb," as if he'd just discovered a new human quality, and sat down on the arm of the chair so that Janie was squeezed comfortably between him and her mother. "Now listen, Jan-Jan," said her father, "it's not as bad as you think, it's really not. Right?" he said to Mom. She gave him a long look and smiled with one side of her mouth.

"No, not that bad. Couldn't be *that* bad."

"But now comes the tough part," he went on. "We did say 'divorce' to each other a few months back. You know, Janie, sometimes it does happen that two people decide they don't want to go on living with each other. We said it and we meant it at the time, as something to think about. We were pretty upset—well, mad—at the time. And since this isn't the evening for kidding people, I'd say there are still some things that bother us and maybe have to be worked out. But, Honey, we aren't dividing up the silverware just yet."

"Not after the last few days," Mom broke in. "Listen, darling, I guess you understand I went up there to see Gram so I could think about a few things I never seem to have time for when I'm at home. You know what a good place the end of the dock is for that. So I sat on the end of the dock and tried to think, and I did think some, I guess, but mostly I just felt miserable because I missed you so much and even the island didn't seem right without you and Daddy. I think if Gram hadn't been there, or maybe if old Molly weren't so pig-headed, I would have turned right around and come back the next day. But I did stay, and I guess I'm glad. I hope you understand that Daddy and I both know we made a mistake not to tell you how we were feeling, and let you reach all the wrong conclusions. Maybe we just didn't realize how grownup you're getting to be."

Uncle Arthur had hardly said a word, but now he made a harrumphing sound and said, "May I put in a word here?"

They all looked up. "Okay, big brother," Dad said. "You're entitled. I seem to recall we're related."

"Well then, Ken, Molly, look here." Uncle Arthur's face was pink, even though there was a nice breeze from the garden window. "You can't imagine how much I'd rather stay out of this, but it does seem to me that you're not really getting down to the central issue. We've heard a lot about, ah, the way things have been in the past, and how you aren't going to let them go on the same way in future, but we haven't really cleared up anything about the roots of the situation. I mean, I hear a lot of references to Ken's job and this paper, but what's that all about? Is it even the main issue?" Suddenly he seemed to realize that he had gotten to his feet and was looking down at the three of them like a policeman giving a traffic ticket. He bent down quickly to pick up Maxim and added over his shoulder, "None of my business, of course. But since we did raise the question..."

Now it was Dad's turn to stand up, hitching one hand into his pants pocket and fiddling with his key chain as he walked to the window. He looked up at the sky as if he rather hoped there would be a tornado or a flying saucer to point to, but the little patch of rose behind the aurelia tree was blank and he shrugged his shoulders. "Man," he said, "you always *did* go for the tough ones. I suppose it's hard to talk about because it's so simple on the surface. Only, we each see it as simple in a different way. We got that far in our talk this afternoon. You see, they're in the market for an area supervisor and, frankly, I think I could do the job, but I just damn well don't know if I want to. Of course, it would be a change, as Molly points out. I know she thinks I ought to do it. We talked about it last spring and I agreed to spend the summer on the paper, but blast it, the topic bores me cross-eyed and we were doing okay the way we were, as far as I could see. I told her last winter she shouldn't push herself so hard at the decorating, but she doesn't seem to see that my way either.

"Art, I guess you're right; it's not just this one job we're talking about. I just don't quite know what it *is*. One thing's for sure, though. We've taken enough of this out on Janie. Like the man said in the asylum: just because we're crazy doesn't mean we're stupid. I don't quite know how we'll manage, but there's going to be more talking and less faking it. Agreed?" He looked at Mom, who nodded without saying anything, and then he laughed a little and pushed himself away from the windowsill. "Speaking of talking, I haven't made such an oration since that famous debate I referred to. Art, I could really use that beer you offered us a while ago."

Everyone was smiling and moving around as if to show that something was over. "Hey, Dad," asked Janie, "what was this debate, anyway?"

Did the words really settle anything? She didn't know, but it was easy to join in their feeling of relief.

Her father put out a long arm and pulled her up against him. "The debate? Oh, nothing so much, really. We were supposed to be in a statewide contest, all the way over in Akron, but when I got there I couldn't find my speech and then my partner got appendicitis half an hour before we were due to go on. Was I ever terrified."

"So what happened?"

"Well, luckily I had a big brother who drove back home and found the rough draft of my speech for me."

Uncle Arthur was coming back from the kitchen with three glasses of beer and some ginger ale for Janie. "Oh yes," he interrupted. "I drove back for the speech all right. I really burned the road, too, but I got stuck behind a hay truck and the debate was half over by the time I got there. Your father was up on stage doing his part and Myra Whatsit's and our Mama was sitting

219

in the front row crocheting the fringe of her best stole into an afghan she was making. He came in fourth, too. Out of fifty-three teams."

Mom looked over at Dad and her smile was a real one now. "You farmboy faker," she said. "Letting a poor Boston Irish lass try to argue with you, and the smooth debater's tricks as thick on your tongue as the hair on a cowhide. Come on now," she added. "It's late and we're all going out for pizza. Yes, Arthur, even you. A little ordinary, nongourmet food will be good for you."

Then they all went to Goldberg's, where extra cheese really means extra cheese, and Janie decided her uncle's stomach couldn't be too much insulted, because he ate a whole pizza and the part of Mom's she didn't finish.

Later they all went back to Uncle Arthur's to get Janie's suitcase, because she *was* supposed to go home that night after all. "Of course you are, darling. What did you think?"

But Mom didn't ask that again after she saw Janie's corner of the Whosis Room—Big Bear and Baby Bear on the bed, the shell collection on the bureau, the books on the table, and Sargie's picture hung on the post of the upper bunk. "Oh, sweetheart. It looks as if you were planning to stay a year. It looks as if you'd evacuated a bombed-out house."

"Well?" said Dad, and that was all he said. But he was the one who helped Janie pack while Mom sat on the bottom bunk talking to Uncle Arthur and sometimes patting Big Bear.

They had already started down the street with Janie's suitcase, heading for the cabs on First Avenue, when Janie stopped dead. "I forgot something," she explained. "I just have to get it. I won't be a minute." Turning, she ran back and up the steep steps to her uncle's front door. He must just have been on his way up to the study because, although all the lights were out in the living room, he opened the front door the moment she knocked. Maxim was draped over his shoulder, head end first, and in Uncle Arthur's hand was one of the globe-shaped, stemmed brandy glasses Mom and Dad had given him last Christmas.

"I forgot something," she explained again, feeling suddenly strange in the dim hallway. She knew just where it was, however, the sketch pad propped beside the big leather chair, where he had put it down that morning. She went and got it quickly.

"I wondered whether you wouldn't want that," he said. "I would have mailed it to you tomorrow."

"Oh yes, I'll want it. There are always things to draw. Even right around home, I mean. It's a good thing to do, sometimes."

Tall and bulky, rounded and precise, he looked down at her over the top of his half-glasses. "So you under-stand that, do you? That's good. Just remember, people don't always . . ." It was the first time she had ever seen him grope for words. "I mean to say, it isn't always possible for people to feel or do things the way they say they will, no matter how much they'd like to. When you can't get away from that, it sometimes helps to—draw pictures."

Hugging her pad, Janie sidled past him in the narrow hallway. There was no need for hugs and kisses, she knew, and the polite words had all been said at Mom's direction. Still, she wanted to do something to thank him—because he had cared enough to warn her and known she would understand. With the door already open and the street light shining through in a long white slant, she turned and asked a question. "Could I come back sometime? I mean, just me? If it seemed like a good idea?"

It might have been a pleased flash of his glasses or just Maxim's gold, unwinking stare she saw as he replied, "Oh yes. We'd like that. I'm always here, you know. Except, of course, when I'm away. At any rate, I always come back. Goodnight, now." She didn't hear the door close behind her until she was at the bottom of the steps and trotting toward the taxi that had stopped for her parents on the corner.

When they got home it was late, but before Janie went to sleep she leaned far out of her bedroom window and twisted her neck until she could see the head and shoulders of the stone griffin standing on the roof. Funny, two months ago she hadn't dared lean out far enough to see him. Now it was nothing; she'd been in much more dangerous places. "Hi, Griff," she said in her head. She knew by now that there were no limits to her ability to call him. He could have come planing down to her on gilded wings there in her bedroom, or on the jetty on Dixon's Island, or inside a locked bank vault. Griff and his world had been a good place for her, most of the time. But there was Sekhmet—and the power of the great dance. Sekhmet was as much a part of that kingdom as Griff. For now, she would leave them alone.

The two worlds were not so different after all. There was no way of being sure what would happen in either of them. No safety belts, but no inevitable disasters, either. Stone is patient, she thought, but maybe so are people. "Goodnight, old griffin," she called, and then she let him answer.

"Goodnight, little one. Remember how the underside of a bridge sounds, and the way the city looks like a trailing scarf of black silk below you. Remember the uses of circles, remember how a centaur's body joins his back, remember that Lestoil is all right for cleaning statues. Most of all, remember that the Stonefolk will always be here for you."

"I know that," she said, and climbed into bed.

About the Author

Georgess McHargue grew up in New York City, was graduated from Radcliffe College, and has been an editor of children's books. She is the author of over a dozen books for children, including *The Impossible People: A History Natural and Unnatural of Beings Terrible and Wonderful*, which was nominated for the National Book Award in 1973.

She first began to write as a small child—about wholly imaginary creatures. She says, however, *Stoneflight* came "directly out of a New York childhood in which not only the sculptures of the city but the city itself became 'quick' to my imagination. I know many other secrets about the city, such as the fact that there are three petrified hippopotamuses disguised as islands in the East River and an alligator who lives in a submerged streetcar under the Queensboro Bridge."

Ms. McHargue is married and lives in Massachusetts with her husband. She is also the author of a picture book, *Private Zoo*, published by Viking.